MON

Breed
of the
Chaparral

Breed
of the
Chaparral

Nelson Nye

THORNDIKE
CHIVERS

This Large Print book is published by Thorndike Press®, Waterville, Maine USA and by BBC Audiobooks, Ltd, Bath, England.

Published in 2003 in the U.S. by arrangement with Golden West Literary Agency.

Published in 2003 in the U.K. by arrangement with Golden West Literary Agency.

U.S. Hardcover   0-7862-5717-2   (Western)
U.K. Hardcover   0-7540-7353-X   (Chivers Large Print)
U.K. Softcover   0-7540-7354-8   (Camden Large Print)

The text of this Large Print edition is unabridged.
Other aspects of the book may vary from the original edition.

Set in 16 pt. Plantin.

Printed in the United States on permanent paper.

British Library Cataloguing in Publication Data available

Library of Congress Cataloging-in-Publication Data

Nye, Nelson C. (Nelson Coral), 1907–
    Breed of the chaparral / Nelson Nye.
        p. cm.
    ISBN 0-7862-5717-2 (lg. print : hc : alk. paper)
    1. Revenge — Fiction. 2. Large type books. I. Title.
PS3527.Y33B74 2003
813′.54—dc21   2003054252

FOR
THE COCHRANES
HAROLD AND HELEN

Chapter 1

The first time Tune laid eyes on the girl she had her back to the wall of Madam Belladine's brothel with the clothes half torn from her gleaming body and the look of a tigress in the knife-lifted crouch of her. Tune jumped for the man. The fellow whirled and fired, his slug purring death past the edge of Tune's ear. When Tune caught his balance the girl was gone — gone as swift as the man, gone as quiet, as completely.

That had been Tucson. The *barrio libre*.

This was Oro Blanco, one week and sixty-some-odd miles later. The girl was the same but the man looked different. They were in the mauve shadowed doorway of Riske Quentin's cantina. Tune could not catch the drift of their whispers, but their postures, their gestures, were unmistakable. Threat stood in each line of the man's angry shape.

The girl's head lifted sharply. Her glance met Tune's.

The effect of that look was like a touch

of pure lightening.

Tune breathed deeply, darkly staring.

She was clad in the rags of a border gypsy. Bare toes, delicately contoured but fouled with the grime of this dusty road, peeped from the open ends of huaraches. But her eyes were blue — Great God, what a blue! Like the eyes of a child! Like the windy blue of the sunswept heavens. And Tune swung unthinkingly out of the saddle.

He could not have said what moved him into this. Impulse, probably — the quickened urge of piled-up hungers. The girl reacted as swiftly. Relief came into the look she swept him — relief and remembrance, and a pithy kind of a halfway promise that brought him hard up against the man, that put Tune's hand on the burly shoulder and savagely swung the man round to face him.

He was big — that man; lithe and brown as a golden snake. Gold flashed from the lobes of his pendulous ears and his uncropped hair was shaggy and tousled where it showed from under the floppy-brimmed hat. His shapeless shirt was of cotton and, like the cotton drawers that covered his shanks, might once have been white. Straw sandals encased his big, muscular feet and his drawers were kept up by a twist of rough hemp. There was a raveled serape flung across his shoulder.

His left eye drooped in a kind of sour wink.

He didn't waste breath and he didn't waste time. There was a knife in his hand and he dived to use it. Tune swayed from the waist and, as the blade ripped past, put five hard knuckles square against the man's jaw. The man's feet left the ground and he went over backwards. His head struck the step and he lay sprawled there loosely.

Tune looked for the girl. She was gone again. He yanked open the nearest half of the batwings but he did not see her inside the cantina. With an irritable shrug he went back to his horse and climbed into the saddle.

He sent the horse down an alley toward Grankelmeir's stable and was building a smoke when he dropped the makings and did an odd thing — very odd, considering. He loosened the bedroom behind his cantle, thrust gunbelt and gun out of sight inside it; then he retightened the roll and rode on.

He slapped at a fly and scowled irritably. That pair and their business meant nothing to him. Sneak thief and harlot.

But he knew as he thought it they had

not had that look.

That was what bothered him, what kept his mind on them when it should have been taken up with things more concerning him. What if the girl *did* have blue eyes? Like enough there were plenty of blue-eyed gitanas if a man cared to go to the bother of hunting them.

Just the same . . . There was something about the girl's eyes that stuck with him, unquieting the accustomed run of his thoughts. So like a child's! They made angel's eyes out of that kind of blue!

Tune cursed in his throat and pulled up at the stable, a bleak eyed man in a chin-strapped hat who had troubles enough of his own to look out for. He had not come all this hell of a way to be taken and dangled for a plain lack of caution.

He said: "No, by God!" and got out of the saddle.

He was curling a smoke when Grankelmeir's stoop-shouldered shape came out of the fetid gloom of the stable. There was a calm and relaxing feel to this place, in the hay smell and horse smell that rose up to greet him.

He licked his smoke and put a match to it.

"Right smart of gypsies rovin' round this town."

The stableman nodded. "Yeah — worse'n a plague o' rats, them fellers. You figgerin' to stay long?"

Tune had no answer for that one.

Grankelmeir said, "Not aimin' to be nosy. Kind o' rule of the house. It's cash in advance if you're just passin' through, friend."

Tune dug a cartwheel out of his pocket.

The man was reaching to take it when his eyes went, frozen, toward the stable doors.

A man staggered into the sun's bright blaze, coming out of the stable back first. bent over, hands clutching his chest, his breath spilling out in choked, whimpering groans. He collapsed on his face with both arms hugged under him.

He was dead. Just like that. They both knew he was dead by the way he had fallen.

It was the stealth of the thing that beat up Tune's temper. Death lurching out of that peaceful aura. The deceitfulness of it sent a chill up his spine.

Rage growled through his arteries. He went into that stable cat-swift and cat-wary, completely forgetting he wore no gun.

There was nothing to shoot at. No sign of a struggle. No sound of departure. Nothing — But wait! Yes — there was something. Something red and round on the hoof-scarred planking.

Tune bent. He picked it up and stood holding it, stood oddly grim, eying it.

He suddenly thrust it into his pocket and tramped outside with cheeks enigmatic. He turned the man over. Grankelmeir clucked.

It was a South Texas face they were staring down into, sun-bronzed and stubbled with a three days' beard. The face of a man in his middle forties. One accustomed, by its look, to the giving of orders. No common ranch hand.

"Know him?" Tune asked.

Grankelmeir rose and dusted his knees off. He said, "No!"

Without knowing why, Tune knew the man lied.

He made no comment. He reached down, tugged the knife from between the man's rib bones. It was a long-bladed thing, plain of handle. It had no markings.

Tune was like that, bent above the man, holding it, when two fellows came into the yard from the alley; two men in scuffed range clothes, both talking.

Both suddenly stopped.

The taller man stared with a shape gone rigid. The other man's lips curled. Short and broad this one was, almost dark as a Negro, burnt so by the sun and high wind of this country. He said, "I told the fool them sheepmen would fight."

He looked again at the dead man. His glance touched Tune.

A kind of silence fell. The man looked at the knife still held in Tune's hand. He looked a long time at Tune's gunless waist. He turned with a shrug, with a saturnine quirk of his quick-lifting eyebrows. "Come on — come on!" He pulled the taller man after him off down the alley.

Tune's glance came around to find Grankelmeir watching him.

"I don't suppose," Tune said, "you know *those* gentlemen, either."

"Never saw 'em before. Look — do me a favor. Stop by the marshal's and ask him to drop over here."

Tune said, "Tend to your own dead. He's no kin of mine."

The Crockett House was the only hotel. It wasn't much. As Tune came into its dusty lobby a yellow-haired girl broke her talk off short with an irritable glance in Tune's direction. With an impatient swing

13

of the shoulders she wheeled and went through an uncurtained arch to the dining room. At a table by an open window a young fellow, waiting, got up with a smile and pulled out a chair for her.

The place smelled of cabbage. The desk was a rough, scarred pine affair wedged into an alcove under the stairs. The man standing back of it took his scowl off the girl and, with an ungracious jerk of the hand, got down a key and shoved it at Tune on top of the register. "Number Four," he said — "I guess you can find it."

He kicked back his chair and departed.

Tune, looking after him, picked up the key.

Without so much as touching the register he stepped back on the porch and was that way, considering, when a girl's voice said very cool-like and casual, "Just a moment, stranger."

Tune turned without hurry and met her glance through the window.

It was the yellow-haired girl. She had not bothered to rise. She was bending forward. She beckoned imperiously.

Tune went over. He dragged off his hat and then, scowling, replaced it. "Yes?" he said.

The girl's eyes dropped to his unbelted

14

waistline. When they came up they held a pointed interest. Tune cursed the impulse that had shucked off his pistol. He would better have worn it for the unfaded sign of it was plain on his jeans and the lack of it now invited attention.

The girl smiled. "I've got a job for you."

Tune said nothing. He kept his stony-eyed look upon her and his mind, behind it, sort of wondered what manner of woman this was who so brashly would go about employing a gun man.

She said, "We run Clover Cross — cattle. Teal could use another hand. Another *good* one."

Tune's mind turned over that moment at the stable when the dead man had come reeling into the sun with his hands hugged over the knife that had killed him. *I'm involved in this,* he thought bitterly, *whether I like it or not.*

His presence at that stable had dragged him into it. But he did not have to stay dragged into it. He could saddle and ride . . .

The girl, with just the right touch of irony, said: "I suppose you would work if the price were made large enough."

"If I did," Tune said finally, "it wouldn't be for no petticoat."

Excitement lay in her looks for a moment. Then anger spread its dark flush on her checks; and that was when Tune turned his back and left her.

He stepped onto the boardwalk. His glance stopped at a store in a false-fronted building of sun-cured pine. It was four doors down and had the one word *Mercantile* spelled in bleached paint across its front.

Tune, watchful and wary, stepped into the street, a tall gaunted man with a saddle-bound stride whose care was the cost of continued liberty. He thought: *two years of this business can change almost anyone.* He was changed.

He was not a laughing man any more.

One of these days the law would catch up with him. It was the logical, the inevitable end of all this dodging and hiding. He regarded himself as a man without illusions. He knew he had ought to get out of this town. Two men had seen him holding that knife. One would have been entirely sufficient.

He crossed the Mercantile's porch. He was about to step inside the establishment when the blue-eyed gitana came out of an alley and stopped beside him. She was watching him gravely with her look of a child.

Vitality shaped the curves of her body. She had an animal magnetism that got its hooks into Tune's long hungers and unsettled his habits of vigilance and caution.

He let caution slide and looked his fill of her.

Her lips laughed back at him, became abruptly sober. "The button," she said, and put out her hand.

Tune looked at her carefully.

Her expression turned urgent. "Quick! *Andale* — hurry!"

"What button?" Tune said.

She let the hand drop and he saw how responsive her face was to the things that went on in her mind. Her mouth showed disappointment. She said, "The button you found on the stable floor."

They looked at each other appraisingly.

"So you were there, too."

"Will you give it to me?"

Tune said, "No," and saw her eyes darken.

It wasn't just anger. It was a kind of wonder, really. A kind of searching wonder that left Tune on edge and displeased with himself.

He resisted an impulse to give it to her.

Her breasts showed the lift and the fall of her breathing. She wheeled away and, at once, swung back. "Don't you think that's behaving rather headstrong and foolish? The button does you no good — nothing good can come of this business." She said impatiently, "Come, *prala*, give it to me."

Tune shook his head.

She left him abruptly.

He went into the store still thinking about her.

A face came out of the store's dim coolness and Tune said laconically, "Box of forty-fives," and watched the man's glance briefly drop to his waistline. The man turned without speaking and went behind the partition.

The smells of this room brought pungent memories and Tune was a man to whom memory was poison.

He picked up an unloaded forty-five from the counter and was that way, hefting it, when a man's voice behind him said: "What do you reckon to do with that gun, sir?"

Chapter 2

The ghost of amusement touched the set of Tune's mouth.

The glare from the street left the man a black shape but Tune would have known that voice at midnight.

He said, "How are you, Lou? Thought you was up in the Tonto country."

The black shape moved forward into the store and, with the change in light, took on depth and character. It became a man, spare and still, ramrod straight, immaculate. Expensive black-and-white checked trousers were neatly pressed as was the black Prince Albert snugging his shoulders. Ash blonde curls set off the stovepipe hat and a heavy gold watch chain crossed his flat middle. His cheeks were clean shaven, pale, expressionless.

"What are *you* doing here?" he said irritably.

"Now, Lou," Tune smiled, "that's all past and done with."

"Nothing's ever done with," the man said bitterly. "I'm the Oro Blanco marshal."

19

"You always did like the shine of a star," Tune remembered; and stood watching him, waiting.

An edge got into the marshal's voice. "Damn it, I don't like this, Dakota. Why did you come here?"

"It bothers you?"

"By God, I don't want you around!" Bitter eyes told the depth of Lou's feeling. "Why, hell! You must be —" He let the rest slough of as the storekeeper came into sight with Tune's cartridges.

The storekeeper said, "What's this I hear about Teal gettin' killed? Wasn't somebody —"

Lou Safford said: "Teal killed himself over at Grankelmeir's stable."

He looked at Tune. They both looked at Tune.

"Sure," Tune smiled, and saw Lou Safford's shoulders relax. "Putting your money into sheep these days, Lou?"

It caught the marshal off guard and he looked his surprise. Then a dark tide of color crept up his neck and his mouth went together like the jaws of a trap. Yet, with all that anger, there was a faint hint of fear at the back of his stare. Tune saw it and marked it and paid for his cartridges.

20

He nodded at Lou and with the box tucked under his arm he went out.

Summer's heat curled off the road — off those scarred wooden planks grayly flanking the store fronts. Even the dust smelled scorched and stifling. On the balls of his feet Tune looked at the town, seeing all the stray movements, guessing much from the guise of things not too apparent. The clink and clank of the hoof-shaper's hammer was a steady and untiring beat in the stillness, rhythmic and natural as the action of the cur before the millinery shop. A saddled roan gelding, ground-hitched by the faded two-color barber pole, was scratching its jaw with a hoisted hind hoof while, a bit farther on, before the cracked and patched front of Riske Quenton's cantina two cowhands, just swung from their horses, were staring open-mouthed at a fast talking third.

Safford came out and stopped by Tune's side.

"Been a long time, Lou," Tune reflected.

Lou Safford said with his gambler's exactness: "One year to the day," and fell ponderously silent. His frowning eyes kept roving the town, kept worrying his mind with the things they saw, kept edgily returning to the trio of punchers before the cantina. "Why did you come here?" he burst out suddenly.

"*You* hadn't anything to do with it."

"I don't care," Safford said. "I don't want you around." His eyes raked Tune, wholly without charity. "What have you done with that precious pistol?"

Tune's glance was amused in a remote sort of way. "I kind of reckoned you'd get around to askin' about that, Lou."

A tenseness showed around the marshal's mouth, but he kept his head, kept a hold on his temper. "I'm tryin' to keep this town quiet," he growled.

"That why you called that killin' a suicide?"

The points of the marshal's cheekbones stood out. Some emotion long bottled inside him exploded. The sudden glint of his eyes exposed hatred uncaringly. "*That's* it!" he snarled. "That's why I don't want you around this town — *you're too goddam nosey!*"

"If you got trouble around here soft-pedaling won't cure it."

"You going to tell me now how to run my business?"

"God Almighty couldn't do that, Lou."

A growl came out of the marshal's

throat. In front of Riske Quentin's a crowd had grown. Men stood three deep around the fast talking puncher. The man's quick words were building an effect. He was waving his arms. He suddenly shouted and the crowd shouted with him. The sound of that shout was unmistakably ugly.

Safford caught Tune's arm. "I'm going to tell you something. That dead fellow, Teal, was the Clover Cross ramrod — they been runnin' this country ever since the Indians. That's a Clover Cross hand there that's doing the jawing. That bunch's all ranch hands — a cow crowd. There's a sheep camp out at the edge of Teal's range; he was over there yesterday laying the law down. Now he's dead. And Birch Alder is shooting his mouth off."

Safford locked his stare into Tune's stare blackly. "That's the story. You keep out of it."

He turned on his heel, a tall grim man with a star on his chest, and stepped into the street. He was starting purposefully in the direction of Quentin's when the sound of a solitary shot crossed the wind. It was impossible to tell where that sound had come from. It passed unnoticed by the crowd at Riske Quentin's, but Lou Safford stopped with his feet wide apart. The fingers of his right hand jerked and spraddled. His head came around with an indrawn breath and his bitter eyes sprang at Tune accusingly.

"You see?" he snarled. "Wherever you are, by God, there's trouble!"

There were other words crowding against his teeth when the whole tight look of the marshal's face altered.

Tune trailed that look to the hotel porch.

Every sound in the street went abruptly still. Across that hush a .45 drove violence.

Two men and a girl stood on the Crockett House porch and one of those men was swaying, falling. It was the young man Tune had seen with the girl — with the yellow-haired girl who spoke for Clover Cross. It was she who stood now, shocked of face, sharp staring, with a white-knuckled fist caught against her red lips while a stringer of smoke curled above the bright gun snout; while the man with the pistol politely said:

"I am sorry, Miss Larinda, ma'am, but not even for you I couldn't take that talk."

Chapter 3

Tune broke his stride and stood stopped in his tracks.

Considering this scene with a closer care, the memory of Safford's words came back. This was what Lou meant. It was none of Tune's business.

He hadn't the knowledge to guess what lay back of it, not even acquaintance with the persons involved. He had no way of judging who was right and who wrong. It might not be the brutal killing it looked. The man who had fired might well have been forced to; things beyond his control may have driven him to it. A man couldn't go by the look of that girl — women were a heap too apt to get rattled; they were too crazy-headed to shape a man's judgment in a time like this. That young fellow's hand had been inside his coatfront.

Tune's mind went back through the months to San Saba. To San Saba in Texas. To a scene very like this. To Sheriff Tom Curry sprawled dead on the floor of

the Carlton House bar. Tune shook his
head to get that picture out of it. The sheriff's hand, too, had been thrust in his
coatfront, and the smoking pistol . . .

They said, anyway, it had been in Tune's
hand.

Sheriff killer!

Tune's jaws went white at the remembrance of that cry. He saw the avid faces
that had ringed him round. A cold sweat
drenched his body like rain as he stood
there, locked on the edge of this dusty road
while the hurrying figures went clamoring
past him to swell that justling throng
round the porch.

Lou Safford was right. This was none of
his never-mind.

He looked toward Riske Quentin's. That
crowd was dissolved, gone scampering to
augment the bunch round the porch rail. It
was ever this way, Tune remembered.
Life's gusty interest in death called all
classes.

He went down to Riske Quentin's and
pushed through the batwings.

He pulled out a chair at an empty table.
The place smelled of rotgut and cheap cigarette smoke. Tune well knew its ways, its
bar and its women, its squinch-eyed,
tough-faced, gun-toting customers. This

was the breed Blackwell Stokes had consigned him to.

Breed of the chaparral.

A violin wailed beside a girl on the platform. It packed her song's maudlin melody with all the wild drear flavor of the hills. With voice and gesture, with an art transcending her lowly station, she was pleading with outstretched arms for someone please to put her little shoes away. So utterly earnest was the pitiful look of her, so heart-rendingly choked were her tones with pathos, three shabby old soaks by the end of the bar set out arm in arm to go to her rescue.

But these things were lost on the man called Dakota. There was a cold chill gnawing the pit of his belly and the bottle the barkeep brought held no comfort. There was no anodyne known that could ease what ailed him, no bar that could bolt the door on his past.

Two years!

The keen eyes in his face were vigilant of things not seen in this room.

He thought of the gun he had cached in his bedroll, of the way of his life since leaving San Saba; and his lips twisted into a hard thin line.

Two years of hiding from the hounds of the law.

Two years of brush running, badges and bullets.

A considerable time when measured by the speed of a hand smashed to gun butt.

The cantina's noise became a faraway sound. The tireless drone of the gambler's voices ran on and on. The clink of hard money, the clack of the roulette ball, became as lost on Tune as the oaths and laughter of the booted men round him.

He sat with memory and his cheeks were bitter.

After some time he roused a little. There was no way of telling if the reward bills had come this far yet. The marshal had not braced him, but that did not signify. He knew Lou Safford for a circumspect man, a gentleman filled with odd shifts and dodges. Lou was not the kind to make the same mistake twice. He had tried for Tune once before, and if they tangled again Lou would hold all the aces.

Lou Safford was right. This was no place for Tune. Everything here was stacked for trouble. In the past two years Tune had seen enough trouble to last him a lifetime. But he kept remembering that young fellow falling. He kept remembering the look of that girl.

But for the look on the face of that yellow-haired girl he would now be riding, would be losing himself with the winds of the desert. His luck could not hold. He knew that. The long arm of the law was bound to catch up with him. And there were things he must do before that time came. There were accounts to be settled — they cried out against staying.

Yet he did not go.

He sat there morosely sprawled at his table, a saddle-whipped man in trail-grimed clothing. A man gaunted by travel and dogged by doom — *that* was the way the look of him struck you. He had the ways of a man who had Death for a trailmate.

All the drives of his nature were urging him back to the grim accounting. To the belated reckoning with Blackwell Stokes for the things which had driven him out of his homeland, for the blackhearted treachery which had hounded him here to this waste of cholla and sand and catclaw, to this hell of green-slimed waterholes where only the wolves and coyotes came, where only the chaparral breed could survive.

But through the urge of these things came that vivid picture — the young man falling, the tragic look of the girl. He could not forget the shocked beauty of that face. With the clean silver brilliance of a daguerreotype her features were vividly etched in his mind. In retrospect there seemed to be about their gentle beauty a strange look of remorse. Perhaps it was but some quirk of memory which gave them that odd, that haunting quality. But it was there in his thoughts of her. He could not banish it. And he could no more go with that face in his mind than he could get back those things the black past had stripped from him.

Price! That was what she had said — "if the price were made big enough." Price! What could *she* know of price, with her crew of hired hands and her thousands of cattle! With her uncounted acres!

No matter, he thought. There were things in this world that a man could not do.

Blackwell Stokes had first shown him that. Blackwell Stokes, his friend, high commissioner at San Saba. How well Tune recalled the sad look of the man, that regretful voice as Stokes had said with deep sympathy, "No, I'm sorry, Tune. This thing has gone too far. Neither repentance nor innocence can reshuffle the cards. Sheriff Curry is dead. You cannot change that. You cannot escape your connection with it. There are powerful factions at work in the land . . ."

Tune ground his teeth and got up, blackly scowling.

It was plain enough the powerful factions were here, too. The demands of that girl had to have their way with him; he could not leave her, or any woman, to face by herself the ugliness he saw shaping up here. For this was the old, unforgettable pattern, and a sly, sly hand was lying light on the reins.

He got out of his chair while the mood was on him, a leather-legged man with a broad sweep of shoulder and a wintry chill in the glint of his look.

Dark-cheeked and solitary he moved through the crowd, through the swirling layers of blue-gray smoke. He was lifting a hand toward the halfleaf doors when a man, shoving in, brought up hard against him.

The man grinned at him tightly. This wasn't an accident.

The man drove an elbow into Tune's ribs and Tune fetched a fist back and let the man have it. Surprise was a flare in hot off-balance eyes and the look of the fellow turned purely wicked as the doors, shoved back by the thrust of his weight, spilled him heavily onto the planks of the porch.

Tune batted the doors and went through them after him.

The man was up on one knee when he saw Tune coming; the gleam in his hand was a lifting pistol. Tune kicked the gun loose, sent it skittering streetward; and the man surged erect and came tearing into him.

Tune let him come, taking the jolt of those blows without feeling them. This was something he could get his teeth into. He hit the man in the belly. He grinned at him toughly. The man's head dropped with whistling breath. Tune fetched him another, full and square on the temple. The man went down on his back and stayed there.

Tune's glance flashed darkly up and around. All the barroom gun toughs stood jammed around him. They were watching him, wondering; and it was one of these wonderers whose look Tune found interesting.

Sudden warning prickled the hair of his scalp. This was a face he had seen before;

the burnt-dark face of the short and broad man of Grankelmeir's alley.

The man smiled thinly and nodded. Then he turned on the balls of his feet and departed; and somebody came with a bucket of water and splashed it across the downed man carelessly, and the crowd broke up.

Tune wheeled his shape in the bright glare of sunlight and struck off toward the porch of the Crockett House. But, midway on his course, something changed his mind and he turned and, instead, went up Grankelmeir's alley.

Someone had been through his bedroll.

With anger dark on his skin he went through his things but found nothing missing. He got out his gun belt and buckled it round him, grimly tying the whang strings that hung from his holster. He got the fresh cartridge box out of his pocket and stuffed the empty loops of his belt, replacing the shells he shook out of his pistol.

He bent his steps toward the hotel again.

There was wildness in this town and he felt it.

Yet the town was no different than a hundred others Tune had been in and out of since he'd gone on the dodge. A border town with the border's stamp plainly, dingily on it. One long crooked street hock deep in dust and two thin rows of false-fronts flanking it. Two lines of tie rails paralleled these, their poles roughly polished by the reins of hitched horses. There were a lot of hitched horses at the tie rails now and a couple dozen wagons helped to clutter the store fronts.

Tune kept to the dusty middle of the road and was uncomfortably aware of things happening around him.

Lou Safford, he thought, had come a far piece since Atchison.

A hulking fellow with a hard and bland face stepped out from the shadow of a dancehall's awning. He looked Tune's way and then eased round a corner.

Tune's glance lifted over the hotel's front. A cold amusement briefly lighted it, for back of a curtained upstairs window some other shy soul was keeping cases. From a shanty with *Minnie's* blazoned redly across it a smile and a shapely arm invited.

The hand on the reins was a knowing, sure one.

Heat curled like smoke from the drifted dust, it puffed with the dust from each forward boot thrust. Smell of frying food reminded Tune he was hungry and he scraped his spurs across the Crockett House porch and bridged its emptiness with lips drawn tight. There were watching men along both sides of the street, but these would not stop ambush from striking him. The feel of this town was an ugly thing.

Tune passed into the dining room.

He took a table with a wall behind it. He removed his hat and mopped the sweat off his forehead. The hasher's tired eyes revealed a shopworn interest. Tune said, "Whatever's handy," and heard her call *"Ham an'!"* through the kitchen doorslot.

A man got up and came and bent over him. "When you're ready to work I'll find a place for you."

It was the short and broad man who had smiled at Riske Quentin's.

"Usually pick my own."

"You'll find it different here."

The man smiled amusedly while Tune shaped a cigarette.

" 'Fraid you're slantin' your talk at the wrong gent, pardner."

The dark-faced man did not answer immediately. He fetched out a plug of very black tobacco, bit off a chunk and stood chewing thoughtfully. He stared through the smoke Tune had wreathed about him and had no need to say what he thought for the shine of that thinking lay plain on his cheekbones. He was a type Tune knew with his shotgun chaps and that blue bandanna knotted tight at his throat.

This man was a gun boss and both of them knew it.

The man finally hauled up his shoulders and spat. "Mebbe you better just ride along, Mister."

Brashly Tune grinned.

The man's eyes grinned back at him.

"This ain't San Saba," the man said. "You mebbe wouldn't be quite so damn lucky here."

Chapter 4

Tune said when the hasher came back with his dinner, "Who was the gent that shot the kid?"

The woman's tired eyes jumped nervously up and met Tune's look with a guarded watchfulness. "Stacey Wilkes," she said finally. "He's the Seven Keys owner."

"And that jigger that just went out of here? That dark faced bird in the shotgun chaps?"

"You must be new around here," the girl said. "Didn't think I'd seen you around before. Just get in?"

Tune smiled at her gently. He put down a cartwheel alongside his coffee cup. "Fellow in the chaps just offered me a job. Forgot to mention what the name of his spread was."

The girl's eyes studied the pink checks of the tablecloth. Her glance touched the coin, touched Tune's face and dropped back again. She took a look at her hands, at their roughness and redness, and rubbed them against the soiled white of her apron.

"That was Crowly, Wilkes' range boss. Quite a friend of the marshal's."

She picked up the coin and went back to the kitchen. Her words lingered with Tune. They kept tramping through him, dragging up memories, disjointed reminders of this marshal, Lou Safford, as Tune had once known him.

Lou had not changed much. This had ever been Lou's nurtured style. The strong against the weak. Where the riffraff ruled you would find Lou as riffraff. Where the law was paramount Lou wore the star — or was able to move it to suit his fancy. The strong against the weak; it had paid Lou dividends.

Yet there was a difference here. Tune considered it carefully. Lou's interest appeared to be geared to the Seven Keys program, yet Lou had himself named Clover Cross largest.

That made things pretty plain to a man who knew Lou.

Tune had known Lou Safford when the railroad boom had been expanding Atchison. Tune had been riding fast in those days, for that was when the chase was fresh and Stokes' star packers had asked no more of fate than to get their gunsights lined on Tune, on this man who had counted Stokes his friend.

Wherever hard cash was to be had from the gullible, there you would find Lou Safford's tent. A river boat gambler, Lou had quit the decks of the great paddle-wheelers for the greater spoils at the "end of steel." As trouble shooter for the construction outfits Tune's path and Lou's had frequently crossed until, one night with his own bare hands, Tune had knocked Lou cold and pulled his tent down over him. Four hours later they had told Tune to travel; the railroad said his job had played out. But Tune understood Safford's friends had brought pressure. They were men in high places.

A smile struck across Tune's lips, hard and thin, and he pushed back his chair and got up from the table. He caught up his hat and went into the lobby.

The natty dressed clerk had his feet on the desk again. He brought them down with an angered abruptness and a scowl clamped the lips around his fat cigar. "It's the custom here to put your name on the register."

"Is it?" Tune said, and went on up the stairs.

On the dim upper landing he paused

39

uncertainly. He wished he had thought to take a look at that register. He could see the door with the #4 on it. He tried his luck with his knuckles on #1.

The door swung open while his hand was still up there.

A stoop shouldered man in batwings stood eying him.

"Maybe I'm wrong," Tune said. He smiled meagerly. "I been coddlin' the notion this was Miss McClain's room. Miss McClain of the Clover Cross."

The man pressed his leather-dry mouth together. His stare went over Tune bleakly. "What business would *you* have with Miz McClain?"

"I guess that would be *her* business, wouldn't it?"

"Oh! Let him in, Ives," the girl's voice said.

Tune moved into the room. The man shoved the door shut. He put his back to it stiffly and his bright, baleful stare stayed on Tune with cocked interest.

The yellow-haired girl was in a rocker by the window. The heat of this room was like a clenched fist, yet the girl's cheeks showed no sign it had struck her. She looked at ease, very cool and just a little bit scornful as she lifted her glance to meet Tune's.

It made him wonder if he'd read this aright. Looks could fool you. That young fellow killed on the porch downstairs might not bear any relationship to her.

She said, "Changed your mind about petticoats?"

Tune shook his head. There was a displeased look in the shade of her eyes, and Tune wondered why this was. He figured she should have been pleased to see him. If she had wanted him once she ought still to want him. And he was a little surprised about one other thing; he could find nothing tragic in the look of her now.

There was something of dislike — even a kind of regret, in the way she sat there and eyed him.

He was a lonely man, and suddenly he knew it; a lonely man with all of a lonely man's preconceived notions. He was a gun slung rider of the far dim trails who had known better things and again desired them. But he was, he told himself, practical also, and this side of his nature turned his look briefly wistful as he saw with a numbing clarity how all his days must be like this, how ever and always he must be an outsider to the good things of life. Bloodshed and violence would tramp by his side through all the last days of his life,

41

he thought. By his own hard stubbornness he had made his bed, and there was nothing left now but to lie in it.

All the lines of his face pulled together then and he left the hat where it was, on his head. He had pride himself, and roughed up by the look of her it kept him from saying what he had come here to tell her. He said instead, "That boy — that young fellow you ate with . . . Your brother, wasn't it?"

"You knew that, didn't you?"

He said: "I've no time to waste kicking words around with you. If the man was your brother, say so."

"Certainly he was my brother! Now what do you want here?"

He gave her back angry look for look. "I've come back to say I'll hire on, if you want me. To hire on like you asked me."

He expected some sharp and furious words from her. As a matter of fact it was the man, Ives, that answered.

"We don't need no damned gun fighters!"

A paleness touched Tune's cheeks and was gone.

The girl said, "Wait! — I'm going to hire him, Ives."

Ives said: "No, by God!" He slashed a

hand down. "You're crazy with grief, girl — you don't know what you're doing. You git into that bed and git you some sleep. If your mind's plumb set on it I'll find you a leather slapper, but it won't be one with the look of this feller!"

A door slammed somewhere downstairs off the lobby and a lift of voice sound reached them and dimmed. Tune's face stayed inscrutable.

The girl said sharply, "What's the matter with his look?"

Ives' weather-scoured cheeks showed an impatient anger. "Look! Teal gits kilt. Your brother gits kilt. Then along comes this feller with a gun to rent out to you." There was plain open violence in the man's look at Tune. "I say it's too damn pat! A kid in three-cornered pants would know better'n to let this guy git in gunshot of 'im."

There was pride in this girl — there was a lot of it, Tune thought, watching the changing pattern of her features. Pride and a will that would have its way. She said, "That's prejudice, Ives. If you've any real reason —"

"Reason! You ask me fer *reason?* Didn't I jest see him gabbing with that damn Jess Crowly! That's reason enough, ain't it? Who is he, anyway? *You* don't know — *I* don't know! But he was there at the stable when Teal got that knife in him, and by God that's enough reason for *me!*"

The girl looked at Tune. She got out of the rocker. She said: "Is that true?"

"This fellow works for you, don't he?"

"You're goddam right I do!" Ives growled hotly. "All the time! Every inch of the way!"

The girl never took her eyes from Tune's face. "You haven't answered my question."

"Sure it's true. I had just got to town. Was putting my horse up. I was standing in the yard talking to Grankelmeir — just fixing to pay him — when your range boss come reeling out of the stable."

"And Crowly?"

"I was downstairs eating. Crowly came over and offered me a job."

She said, "Why didn't you take it?"

"He did," growled Ives. "He's workin' at it, ain't he?"

Larinda McClain's green eyes searched Tune's face.

Ives said, tight and bitter, "A man don't smash one of Jess Crowly's riders an' get clean away without it's been fixed up fer him! Not in this town of Oro Blanco he don't! There was Seven Keys riders all around this guy and not a damned one of

44

'em lifted a eyebrow!"

The girl's look at Tune showed a quick, sharpened interest.

She smiled. "Good! You may consider yourself hired. We'll be leaving for the ranch inside the next hour."

Chapter 5

Ives' whole look was hotly incredulous. His lips fanned out, indescribably bitter. He looked ready to break into violent voice, but his mouth snapped shut without spilling a word. He jerked open the door and slammed it after him.

Larinda McClain's red lips curved again.

She had a generous mouth; and she put up her hands now and swept back the hair that was like spilled gold against the cream of her cheekbones. She said: "That was Ives Tampa. He's taking Teal's place as the Clover Cross ramrod. I guess you know why I'm hiring you, don't you?"

Tune rested a hip on the table and looked at her. "Maybe I'd better hear you say it yourself."

Her glance remained smiling. It became speculative, also.

He said, "You trust Tampa, don't you?"

"Yes — of course. He's loyal. Whatever his faults, that isn't one of them. He's been twenty years running this country's roundups. Dad placed his worth as beyond all argument."

"So you've set him down in a dead man's boots, but you know too well his feet won't fill them."

She pulled up her chin. He watched her take a deep breath. Then she nodded. "There are too many things Ives would never do. Too many things he *couldn't* do. We've got a fight on our hands. I don't mean to lose it."

She stood tall and straight and met his look fairly.

She had sand, all right. She had a courage compounded of things seldom component to a woman's character. She had keenness and insight, and the kind of foresight and determination needed to back them. She had made up her mind, he thought, to fight fire with fire, and she did not want for a right bower in this any man whose hands would be tied by scruples. She had hired Nason Tune because she believed him an outlaw.

It ran through her words. She said, "What do we call you?"

"You hirin' a name or a gun?" Tune asked, and watched her. She didn't get riled.

"We've got to call you something."

"You can call me Dakota."

"Dakota what?"

"Just Dakota," Tune drawled; and he could tell by her eyes his guess had hit close enough.

She considered the brash wintry look of him, nodded.

"Have your horse by the porch inside a half hour."

Tune took his hip off the table. "Don't you reckon you'd better maybe post me a little?"

Her knowing eyes raked the hang of his holster. "I see you've found your gun." She grinned a little; put her hand on his shoulder. "You'll do what you have to do. If it's good for the ranch I'll back you till hell freezes."

Going down the stairs Tune thought about that. When he got to the bottom other things took his notice. The lobby was empty.

Tune went through the door.

Trapped heat off the porch was like a fist shoved against him. A look at the street showed less wagons, more horses. He twisted a smoke and got a match from his hatband.

There were too many men on this street doing nothing.

He struck the match with the edge of a thumbnail. That same left hand cupped the flame to his cigarette. Strong fingers snapped the wood splinter and dropped it.

He had lived too long by the feel of intangibles not to be warned by the look of things now. He considered those round-about men once more and pulled up his shoulders and moved into the street.

The clank of his spurs became loud in the quietness.

A man stepped out of Grankelmeir's alley. The man looked at Tune. Tune saw the man's mossy teeth leer back at him.

This was the fellow Tune had knocked through the batwings. This was the old, old pattern again. There was no need for words — no time for words, either.

The man slashed a hand down and dug for his pistol. The barrel came level as Tune's gun spoke.

Dust jumped out of the man's hand-stitched vest. You could see the man stagger.

He was folding forward like a horse bedding down when a quiet voice said, just back of Tune's elbow: "I'll take that gun, Tune."

Tune!

49

The sound of that name locked Tune in his tracks. He stood utterly still in the dust and the sunlight with his mouth stretched thin and each jerked nerve in his wire-taught body shrieking its urge that he whirl and fire. This was the blind hypnotic impulse inherent in every creature that breathes, waiting only the blood-money cry of the scalp hunter to be at once trans-muted into violence and bloodshed — the wolf urge of the fugitive.

No man moved to hem him in and that, in itself, held its fierce significance. They had been well placed and well chosen.

A harried light flared in Tune's glance as it raked past each closed way of departure. Desire, utterly primitive, pulled down his shoulders as he saw how they waited, soft wooden faced, some drear with an abysmal eagerness akin to the look of a waiting vul-ture. They *were* vultures, really — vulture breed of the chaparral.

Then he saw Crowly's stiff and still shape by the barber pole and knew whom he had to thank for this trap; and strangely, quietly, tight of mouth, he smiled.

"Your pot," he said, and held out his gun by the barrel, without argument.

It caught Lou Safford off balance. He stared, incredulously, upset, unbelieving, unable to credit such a tame surrender. "What's this?" he said; and then quickly, irritably: "I'm not falling for no trick like that! Throw it down in the dirt!"

Tune let the pistol drop. Safford's look became ludicrous. "I'll be goddamed!" he said. "I'll be goddamed! *Yellow!*"

"I expect some would call it that," Tune smiled.

Safford's look grew distrusting. "I don't get this, Dakota. You know what'll happen if you go back to San Saba —"

"Maybe somebody's kidding you."

"I guess not." Safford shifted his body. The memory of Atchison rolled across his pale cheeks and he said with his eyes gone entirely vindictive: "When you get to San Saba they'll put a rope round your neck. They'll put a rope round your neck and that will be the end of you."

"San Saba," Tune grinned, "is a long way off."

"You think so? Better take another look at your hole card."

"Lou," Tune said, "this is beginning to get funny."

"Why, you goddam fool!" Safford gritted. "Do you *want* to get hanged? That fellow's got friends. They'll make short work of you."

"For defendin' my life? Why, the man had his gun clean out of leather —"

"My God!" Safford said. "I ain't talking about *him!* It's the man they just found under your bed! Crowly's boss — *Stacey Wilkes!*"

Chapter 6

Like most big outfits of that time and place, Clover Cross had been founded on bloodshed and violence and all of its days had seen their full share, but until last fall none of that blood had ever splashed on its doorstep. Last fall its founder, Tim McClain, had been killed.

A fire-eating Irishman Big Tim had been, one who seldom called anything a spade but a spade. He had called Stacey Wilkes a *goddam thief!* and Mr. Wilkes had promptly drawn pistol and shot him. That was not the end of the business. It was just the beginning. It was still going on.

These were her thoughts as Larinda McClain, after Tune's departure, went back to her rocker and sat with her composed green eyes casually roving the street while she awaited the return of her irascible range boss.

Stacey Wilkes, she recalled, was of Southern extraction. Rumor hailed him from Shreveport in the early '60s — for his health, he had said; and that was mostly true. When a connoisseur and past master of dueling threatens your life in the gray light of dawn it becomes a matter of health to depart somewhat sooner.

Texas had been the habit in those days — the "fashion" one might almost have said. *"Gone to Texas"* described a lot of folks' moving; but Wilkes had thought Texas a little too close and had kept on riding. It would seem Arizona had pleased him better. In that vast desolation surrounding Oro Blanco he had shucked off his saddle and gone into the cow business. There are some who might tell you he'd have need of his saddle, but these lack perception. Wilkes showed that a personal saddle need play no part in a career made prosperous by longhorn cattle. It was inevitable, in the natural course of events, that he and Big Tim, Larinda's father, should clash.

After Big Tim's death, consensus of opinion thought the feud would die out, but consensus hadn't reckoned with the Clover Cross range boss, one Teal, a casehardened citizen from the gunsmoke end of Texas. Teal did not wait for any grass to grow under him. He struck back at Wilkes while the iron was hot. He mislaid forty head of Wilkes' best saddle stock. He did a number of other things a little less openly.

Wilkes offered bonuses — even trafficked with outlaws, but all to no purpose. Teal's depredations continued until no man in the country dared lift hand against him.

Naturally, Clover Cross prospered.

Mr. Wilkes did not. His pride was touched. There was ribald laughter when his name was mentioned. Laughter ate into Wilkes' soul like acid. Teal ate into Wilkes' pocketbook. Wilkes became desperate.

Larinda did not know quite how it had happened, but suddenly the Clover Cross luck petered out. Teal's raids went haywire. Clover Cross began losing men; some were killed, a few quit, several of the best suddenly turned up missing. So did a bunch of the Clover Cross livestock. And in her own mind Larinda blamed it all on Jess Crowly. Short and broad Jess with his dark burnt face and taciturn ways who had come out of nowhere to be the Seven Keys range boss.

Jess Crowly was taciturn. But when he opened his mouth he never had to dig round for any special language to express his meaning. He was cooly efficient without brag or bluster. Old Stumpy, the outfit's cook, could have told you about Jess Crowly. Old Stumpy was handy when Crowly arrived.

It was along in the fall, about grass cutting time, that the dark faced Texan rode into the ranch. Around three o'clock of a hot afternoon. Wilkes was dozing on the broad veranda.

Crowly rode up and got out of the saddle. He shook Wilkes awake.

Wilkes glared out of his whisky bleared eyes and came out of his chair like an uncoiling sidewinder. Crowly's smile stopped him before he opened his mouth. "I'm Jess Crowly, suh. F'om Texas. Told you been huntin' a ramrod. Wheah do you want I should put my belongin's?"

"Just a minute," Wilkes said. "I ain't hired —"

Something about Crowly's look stopped Wilkes' talking.

Crowly said, "Sho't lives an' sho't mem'ries gen'lly runs hitched togetheh. You had me hired 'fo I eveh left Texas. Fetchin' you right up to date you got a bill with me fo' two hundred dollahs an' fifty-fo' cents. Pay it."

Wilkes took a long close look at the man. "You think I will?"

"Mister, I know it. Five chunks of lead in

this gun all says so."

Wilkes eyed the shine of Jess' teeth and nodded.

In many respects Stacey Wilkes was a fool.

There was nothing of the fool about Crowly.

Wilkes wanted power. Crowly knew how to get it. Crowly knew the sure way to real power was fear.

He got down to the business of making Wilkes feared.

The Clover Cross outfit started downhill.

Three of its best men turned up missing. The wrangler asked for his time and faded. Teal took to drink and turned suddenly blasphemous. He understood what was happening but was powerless to stop it. His choicest traps were sidestepped neatly. He commenced to talk of spies. Ives Tampa suggested he go see Safford; that was when Teal really took to the bottle. Safford was Crowly's friend, and Teal knew it. He was as much Teal's friend as a man could be. Crowly had no real talent for friendship. All Crowly's talent was aimed at accomplishment.

Then the sheep moved in and Teal lost his reason.

Crowly stopped Teal in front of Riske Quentin's.

"Heah you've gone in fo' sheep," Crowly grinned. "Tired o' cattle?"

The lift of Teal's shape was a jerk edged with violence and he wheeled full around with the hate in his eyes blazing out bright and naked. Crowly just chuckled and patted Teal's shoulder.

"You want to watch out fo' them fellers. Might git yo'se'l knifed. Then what's thet Cloveh Cross gel goin' to do?"

And he grinned up into tall Teal's red eyes. "Might betteh sell out whilst she's got somethin' *to* sell — though I'm danged ef I know who would want the spread. Said as much to Misteh Wilkes jest las' night. But Wilkes don't want it. Too run down, he says. Not wo'th the botherin' with."

Teal's look got plain wicked, but some vestige of sense kept his hand off his pistol. With a final dry chuckle Crowly walked off and left him.

It tickled Wilkes plenty when he heard of this play. "By the gods," he declared, "you're a real card, Jess! We'll have them eatin' right out of our hands. We're good as got the spread now."

Crowly shrugged.

"Afteh Teal's dead, mebbe. I don't count

much on it. You got t' do suthin' about thet cub, Stacey — the gel's brotheh. Gittin' notions, he is. Shoots off at the mouth eve'y time he opens it. Called you a thief in Riske Quentin's last night. A *lowdown, sneakin', yeller-bellied chicken thief!* — them's his ve'y words."

He looked across at Wilkes blandly.

Wilkes' cheeks roaned up and he sprang from his chair.

"By Gad, sir!" he echoed. "I won't take that talk! I won't take that talk off no one!" And he grabbed up his gunbelt and clapped it around him.

"Keep cahm," advised Crowly. "He's jest a fool kid. You don't want t' do nothing —"

"By Gad, I'll *kill* the whelp!"

"Now, now — you betteh think it oveh."

Crowly knew the man he was dealing with.

Wilkes was so mad his whole frame shook. The look of his cheeks turned apoplectic. He grabbed up his hat and rushed out of the room.

A door banged loudly.

Crowly loosened his shoulders and sat back, thinly smiling.

Larinda went through her mind very carefully. She had known all along how

59

much weight Ives could take. But he was the logical man to step into Teal's boots, so she'd stepped him into them. "But he's a weak reed," she told herself. She thought of the new hand — that gun hung drifter — and smiled. She felt considerable satisfaction in thinking of Tune.

Hiring the man had been a stroke of real luck. Tune looked brash enough to fill her need and he was shaped to that need by his own past conduct — by that which impelled him to be what he was, a man come from nowhere and bound the same place.

Larinda saw what she wanted very clearly. She believed she saw how to go about getting it.

She went over and looked at herself in the mirror and smiled in a pleased way at what she saw there. Then she pulled on her gloves and was turning to leave when something she saw through the window stopped her.

Dying sun lay like fire along the thrust of Tune's jaw. A piece of loose paper lifted out of the dust and was whirled away on a wind from the mountains. No man moved. None took his eyes from the length of Tune's shape. The receding flutter and flap of the paper left a tightened quiet through which Tune scanned his chances without illusion.

The hate of this town could not be mistaken.

Tune looked at Safford. "What was Wilkes doing upstairs under my bed?"

"My God!" Safford said. "The man's dead. With his throat cut."

"And you think I killed him."

"If you didn't," Safford said, "you better start praying. I won't say you had no cause," he growled, lifting his voice up. "Considering San Saba you had cause aplenty. But you ought to know, Tune, that a man can't take the law into his own hands. And that knifing stuff — it don't go around here."

Tune smiled at him thinly.

"I'm afraid somebody's been loading you, Lou."

"Not me. Not this time." Safford dipped his head and stood watching Tune brightly. "Not this time," he said dryly. "Stacey told me about you. About you murdering that San Saba sheriff. And now you've murdered Wilkes trying to hide it."

He made the accusation loudly but there was an undercurrent of fretting unease in the way of his standing, in the way his bright glance kept picking at Tune.

Tune said nothing. He got out the makings and rolled up a cigarette. Every jaundiced eye on that street tabbed its progress and, while they were doing so, Tune found the one thin crack in this business.

There was a gun hawk posted on the porch of the Crockett House; another pair weighted the steps of the Mercantile. Jess Crowly was lounged by the Frenchman's barber pole and, off down the other way in front of Riske Quentin's, two more dark shapes stiffly stood in the sunset.

There were other men watching but Tune ignored them.

There was nobody showing in Grankelmeir's alley.

That was the crack, with its mouth twelve paces from Tune's trapped station. Twelve paces well covered by the snouts of five pistols.

And Lou Safford, the marshal, would have good straight shooting for a clean fifty feet if Tune crowded his luck and tried to get down it.

Bait!

Left deliberately empty to lure him into it.

Lou's love of caution had given Tune this choice. It would look better for Lou if Tune died escaping.

Lou said, and strain was a harsh ground edge in his talking: "If you don't want to swing you better pick up that pistol."

"Sure you want to go on with this, Lou?"

"Damn you, Tune!" Safford shouted. "I'm wearin' a badge! I can't traffic with outlaws!"

"Well, well," Tune said. "You've come a long way since Atchison."

He smiled at Lou then, a smile bleak as malpais; and all the bantering ease fell out of him and he banged his words like bullets at Safford. "You are just a cheap little coyote, Lou, with your lips peeled back because you run with a wolf pack. But you ain't got the guts to *be* a wolf. When the going gets rough you'll slink for timber — and it will get rough, Lou. When I'm roped into something I play for keeps."

"Pick up that pistol!" Safford yelled, half strangled.

One of the pair on the Mercantile's steps growled, "Yappin' won't kill him. Throw your lead into him."

That had been Safford's plan. He had tried to work up to it.

Hate was a bitter bright look in his eyes. Desire for destruction was pounding him, spurring him, shoving him fiercely; but there was no satisfaction left on his cheeks

63

and there was no comforting sureness left in him, either. A man was burnt in the heat of those moments, and that man was Lou; and every eye on that street that was watching him saw it.

Another full moment Safford stood there with that beaten incomprehensible look on his features. Balked rage was in the cant of his shoulders and rage was a consuming fire inside him, but Lou had lived too long with caution. He was done in this town. He had picked this place and he had been left holding it. The wolves would not feel quite the same any longer.

He threw his leaden-eyed look around. A wind inside him puffed out his cheeks. He kept his look away from the barber pole.

"Jail's at the end of this street," he growled. "Get movin'. Get movin'." He shoved at Tune bitterly.

Chapter 7

Larinda McClair turned away from the window with something akin to impatience in her look. It had ever been this way, she remembered. The old days were gone but their flavor lingered, staining yet this land's activities. And the old ways lingered, changed but little. Death still slunk by the side of life and so it would always be, she thought, for this was the same drear story, same country, blood and hungers that had staged the hectic past.

She must watch her step.

This was a desperate game she played, a long-odds game in no-limit country where law was a thing you strapped in a holster and death lone reward for the man who failed.

She must not fail. She *would* not!

Boots came up the creaking stairs and briefly stopped before the door, and the door was opened. Jess Crowly came in and shut it after him and settled his weight against it while his knowing glance played over her cheeks and openly admired the curves of her body.

He gave her a darkly taciturn smile.

She put her words at him coldly. "What do you want?"

Crowly's smile continued. "Jest wanted to tell you. It was a good idee, but it didn't come off. And the' won't none of 'em come off long's you play 'em against me. Might's well make up yo' mind to it."

"Did Wilkes send you up here to tell me that?"

"You reckon I'm playin' houn' dawg fo' *Wilkes?*" Crowly said to her finally: "Stacey Wilkes is dead."

"Dead!"

Her eyes showed a sharp curiosity, but it was not concerned with the Seven Keys owner. She was marveling at this tough-featured Texan who had pulled Seven Keys from the dust by its boot straps. He was big — though not in the same way that Tune was big; he was shorter than Tune and considerably darker. He was heavier, more massively framed with his wide brawny shoulders and hair matted chest. Power was inherent in the man's every gesture. He was a masterful man, and no one knew much about him.

She found the look of his eyes could make you tingle.

Abruptly she remembered what Jess Crowly had said.

"Dead!" she repeated, and her glance came up sharply.

He saw the sudden dark glint of her eyes and he shook his head at her solemnly. "You ought to keep track of what yo' hired hands do."

Larinda said, "Whatever in the world are you talking about? If you've something to say to me, say it and get out of here."

"I say Wilkes is dead in this hotel with his throat cut. The marshal's takin' yo' new man to jail fo' it. That plain enough?"

"*My* new man?" She looked at him blankly.

But Crowly grinned. "Yo' new man. What I said, ain't it? No need to play hide an' seek with me, gel. I'm talkin' about Tune — thet drifteh, Dakota."

Her intention had been to deal coolly with this man, to hold herself above him. But how had *he* known she had just hired Dakota?

Crowly saw the break of that thought in her features. He grinned brazenly.

"Betteh unpin yo' hopes from these driftehs an' hitch yo' wagon to a man thet's goin' places — to a man thet will *stick*. To *me*," he said, and crossed the room and was suddenly before her.

He heard the quick pull of her deepened breathing and his eyes grinned into her eyes understandingly. He saw the rise of her breasts and excitement changed the shape of his face and he put out a hand and touched her lightly.

He stood perfectly still with his eyes locked on hers; and then he took a deep breath and pulled her to him, pulled her hard against him and put his mouth hard against her mouth and kept it there until her hands jarred up and shoved him back.

She stood with her shape filled with tumult, watching him. Her eyes looked bigger and darker. They told Jess Crowly what he wanted to know. He shrugged and smiled and stepped back away from her.

She said with an attempt at her old composure, "taking quite a lot for granted, aren't you?" and an angered look jumped into her stare and, when he would have reached for her again, she knocked his arms down.

"All right," he growled, and stepped clear and put his broad back comfortably against the wall. His grin came back and changed the dark look of him. He said with a gusty confidence, "We could go a long ways, me an' you, gel."

"Maybe I like it here —"

"Sure — sure. What I mean. Cloveh Cross. We could make it the biggest spread in this country. The *only* spread! Hell!" he said boldly, "the ain't hardly nothin' me an' you couldn't do — togetheh."

She reached up and tucked in the edges of her hair. Her look was soft; she was smiling. "I think we'll talk again. You had better go now, I'm expecting Ives Tampa."

He took another deep breath, still watching her. Then he jerked his head in a nod and went out.

They were passing the store, Dakota Tune and the marshal, when a horse came around a far building before them. The girl in the saddle was the blue-eyed gitana. Tune kept his face blank but his thoughts commenced building. Ideas came crowding as he watched the girl slide out of the saddle and carelessly toss her reins at the hitch rack. She went at once up the steps and entered the dwelling.

Tune sent another edged look at the horse. A big yellow claybank, long legged and rangy. There was plenty of bottom tucked away in that home. Tune wasn't guessing — he *knew*. It was his horse. He could see the bulge of his bedroll plainly.

This was no accident. This was planned. Another trap?

Tune studied Safford from the corners of his eyes. The marshal was paying no attention to the horse. No interest canted the set of his features. They were bitterly blank as pounded metal. They belonged to a face hacked out of flint.

And Crowly was gone from his place by the barber pole.

Four of the others fell in behind Safford who tramped back of Tune with a naked gun. Tune knew these fellows weren't going for a walk.

Once again he looked over his chances.

It could be a trap. It could be one more slick scheme of the marshal's to rid them of Tune in a way that would afterward look quite legal. Legality was a complex of Safford's makeup.

Tune thought about that.

There were times when a man found life good and used caution. There were even occasions for shrewdness and stealth. But there were times — and this looked like one of them — when it were best to forget all that and act.

They would pass within ten feet of that horse.

Tune walked with his head tipped forward, apparently fully absorbed with his thinking. The lines of his shoulders looked dejected; but his eyes were small as they roved the street and the slant of his lips was hard as a well chain.

Droning flies filled the still-hot air with their clamor. The sun's last light came no lower than the warped looking chimneys of these flimsy shacks. Soon full dark would roll over this land.

They approached the horse. It was now or never.

Blindingly sudden Tune appeared to go loco. He threw up both hands with a startled yell and dropped flat down on his knees and elbows. Safford, screaming one maniac curse, slammed terrifically into him and pitched sprawling headlong. Tune snapped the pistol out of his hand and whipped Lou grimly across the head with it. He whirled to his feet and fired twice swiftly. Three of the four behind him scattered; the fourth man was hit and stayed where he dropped.

Tune snatched up the reins and dived into the saddle. The rangy claybank lunged into action. Three scattered gun fighters dug for their pistols and lead was a cold thin whine past Tune's shoulders. They went careening around a corner, into an alley between two buildings and the gun-fire and cursing died behind them and flight was a cooling wind in their faces.

Tune rode into the McClain yard at day-break.

Chapter 8

A man came out of a chair on the porch and stepped into the yard with a Spencer rifle. The man was Ives Tampa, and dislike was a stain spread over his cheekbones.

"Turn that horse and ride out of here."

"Maybe you didn't hear the boss say I was hired?"

"We're not hirin' outlaws. Turn that horse and ride out."

"I think not," Tune said. He put his hands on the horn and considered Ives calmly.

The range boss' mouth twisted into a crease. "Ride out!" he said. He lifted the rifle. "Ride back to the Seven Keys where you belong!"

The screen door suddenly opened behind him and Larinda McClain came out and stopped, stopped with an audible intake of breath, the sight of Tune changing her look completely. "Why, I thought . . . I thought you were in jail," she said.

"It don't have to disappoint you, ma'am,

I will be, likely. Soon," Tune said.

Color briefly touched her cheeks and vexation put its mark on them. She considered him intently while the shading of her eyes grew darker, and she did not use the words she first thought of. Instead, watching Tune, she spoke to Tampa. "This man's going to work for us. Put him down as *Dakota*. His job with the ranch will be strayman —"

"Why don't you hire Jess Crowly?" Ives said.

Larinda swiveled a look at him. "Perhaps I shall."

"Now look —" Ives growled, refusing to believe that. "I'm prob'ly old-fashioned. I don't like outlaws. I'm prejudiced as hell. But I'm goin' to tell you I've been around this country, man an' boy, and I've yet to see the owlhooter that ever done anybody any good. When the goin' gets rough they'll slide out on you. They'll leave you holdin' the hot end of the iron. If you can't trust a man what the hell good is he?"

Larinda said, faintly smiling, "According to your argument he wouldn't be here at all."

But Ives waved that aside. There was a doggedness about him that would not be sidetracked. "Use your eyes, girl! The

74

feller's a spy! A man don't smash one of Jess Crowly's riders an' get clean away without it's been fixed up —"

"It's been fixed up," Tune said. "I killed him."

Ives just looked at him. He didn't seem to find that worth answering.

Larinda said: "Put his name in the book, Ives."

The ramrod's feelings were a color in his skin. "By God, I won't use him!"

"*I* will," the girl said. "He will take his orders direct from me. There are ways to this thing you don't understand, Ives. Wars are the same no matter where you fight them. There is no fairness in it. Seven Keys wants control of this country. They will not control me! When brute force is brought against me I will meet it with brute force."

Ives said, "So there's ways to this fightin', is there? Ways I don't understand, eh? Well, you'll learn your lesson but it will be too late. This Seven Keys spy will dig your grave — the same grave he digs for Clover Cross!"

"You take care of the ranch work, Ives. I'll look out for Clover Cross."

Larinda looked at Tune and smiled. "I'll talk with you inside, Dakota."

Ives Tampa's eyes showed dark, inscrutable. Tune watched the boss tramp away and there was respect in Tune's regard of the man. Respect, and a kind of pity.

The girl led the way to her office and closed the door behind them. She tossed her hat in a corner and shook back her yellow hair. She faced Tune much as a man might have done, cold purpose holding her shape erect.

Morning sun, flowing in, threw its light against her. She was something to look at, and Tune's eyes said so. "Ives," she said, "was right about one thing. That Seven Keys crowd is a pack of killers. It's a *bravo brand*. We fight or we fall. I have no intention of falling."

Tune watched her, keeping his thoughts to himself.

"You don't quite approve of me, do you?"

"When you want something," Tune said, "fight for it."

She searched his face. She turned a little away from him. He was struck again by her fullness, by the deep and womanly ripeness of her. She was a cup filled clear to brimming and the look of her hit him hard.

He halfway started to move toward her, then he realized his unfitness and stopped.

He locked his arms behind him, but he could not lock back his words that way. They were out and gone before he could catch them. "You're a brash and handsome woman, 'Rinda — too brash and too handsome for your own good, probably. I have never met a woman like you."

Her eyes came up from behind dark lashes. "Do you always talk to women that way?"

Color came into Tune's cheeks. He was embarrassed. Then he scowled and said gruffly: "I seldom bother to speak with women," and color touched *her* cheeks briefly, and she took her eyes away from him.

She drew a long breath. She turned in the way she had turned in the mirror. "Let's keep this on a business basis." She stepped back and lowered a hip to the edge of her desk. "We've got five men left from a crew of twelve. Our oldest hands; we can probably trust them. But they won't go out of their way to hunt trouble. Hunting out trouble is going to be *your* job." She paused, took another long breath and said: "I want those damn sheep moved. I want you to go over to that camp — What's the matter?"

"Ain't that what Teal did?"

She stood still a moment searching his face again. She moved away from the desk and went over to the windows and stood looking into the sunbaked yard.

"What would you have me do?" she asked finally, and when he did not answer she came back and faced him. She stood close before him and observed how her nearness put pressure into the corners of his mouth. "What would you have me do?" she repeated. "Quit and crawl out like a yellow cur? You think that would become me? You want me to throw up the ranch and get out of here?"

"It's your place," he said, "and your problem."

"You're a real help, aren't you!"

Tune looked at her then. "Wanting has nothing to do with reason. If you want a thing bad enough, sense has no part in it. It's something inside you like a lash or a spur that drives you on and won't ever be done with you."

She continued to watch him, green eyes still questioning.

He said, "If you want a thing bad enough, fight for it!"

She smiled at him then. "I intend to."

When the day's heat finally slacked off a

little, Tune got off his bunk and stepped out into the evening glare. He filled a bucket with water at the creaking pump and soaked his tousled head in it and, afterwards, felt better.

His glance passed round the empty yard, noting the horses in the pole corral, aware that Ives Tampa's mount was there and considering the fact in relation to himself. Then his restive gaze traveled off to the mountains.

Blue they were and hazed by distance, serenely aloof to man and his problems. The mountains did not care whether he lived or died. What difference to them if this ranch changed hands? They would be as they had been since Time's beginning, little altered by man's noisesome passing. There was a power in this country, the power of indifference.

He went to the cook shack and ate some cold meat scraps with his glance turned inward and backward, considering accounts that were yet unsettled, looking over each facet of this Clover Cross wrangle in terms of its relationship to the persons involved.

It was, after all, just the same old pattern. The same lusts still struck sparks from folks. The same greeds urged to thievery, the same desires to violence. The world, he thought, did not change much. Only the methods varied.

He was not surprised by Safford's non-appearance. Lou Safford was a man Tune understood. He would be busy now patching up his conduct, but he would not forget and he would not forgive. He had made a play that had not come off. It had lowered Lou's standing in the eyes of his fellows; but maybe the power that was back of this setup would not care for too strong a badge toter. In any event there was bound to be more of the same before long. There would be reprisals, repercussions. That business of yesterday would not long go unanswered. Lou Safford was merely biding his time. That Lou had no authority outside of town meant nothing. When the iron was hot again Lou would strike — or the power back of Lou would.

Tune nodded. This was San Saba all over again. San Saba dressed up and refurbished a little.

Jess Crowly had known all about San Saba — his words in the restaurant were proof of that. But *how* had he known? Who *was* Crowly? Where had *he* come into Tom Curry's death? What part had *he* in Tune's flight from justice? Had Crowly been someway involved in that deal? What was Crowly's place here?

Tune wheeled with an impatient lift of the shoulders and went outside, went across to the horse pens. He stood looking over the horses awhile and then turned and found Ives Tampa watching him. No catchable expression curbed Tampa's cheeks but his tireless eyes sucked up every movement and the thumbs of his hands hung over his gun belt. Tune wondered with a tempered amusement how long it would be until this man's black notions bred results in gun smoke.

Tampa stood against the pole corral and watched while Tune roped out his horse. He was still there, watching, when Tune finished saddling. He was still there when Tune rode away.

The sheep would be somewhere near the southwest boundary; at least the sheepman's camp was there — Lou Safford had told Dakota that yesterday. It was possible, of course, that the sheep had been moved, but they would probably be in that general direction. Sheep were not given to traveling fast. Sheepmen did not leave strays behind for a strayed-away sheep was a dead sheep. Sheep were born with the will to die and Tune thought it likely they would get their wish hereabouts. Another thing: Sheepmen seldom moved without backing, seldom came into a cow country this way. So it must have been Wilkes who had brought them in here. Part of the Seven Keys plan to smash Clover Cross. After all, it mattered little who owned these sheep. They had been brought in for a purpose and, now that Wilkes was dead, what would Jess Crowly do with them? Lose interest?

No, he would follow up Wilkes' plan very probably. Push the game to the bitter end.

All across the West things like this were shaping up as cattle barons and would-be barons fought tooth and nail to increase their holdings against that time when the law should step in. This age was violent, an age of transition. Woe to the man who stood in greed's way.

And woe to the girl left alone with a ranch that was bigger than many a seaboard state. There would be no peace until the Seven Keys outfit ruled this entire range, or was smashed.

Tune had given some thought to this matter. The man who had killed Larinda's brother was not up to driving this breed of horse — not in Tune's mind. Wilkes had neither the brains nor the vision required to build such a plan or prosecute it. A craftier hand was on the reins than his. And, by this reasoning, Wilkes' death could make little difference to Clover Cross. The plan was to steal this entire region. It was a bid for empire, really. The kind of thing corporations dreamed of.

Was the Seven Keys ranch a syndicate?

It would be. It could be a land and cattle company.

Where had Wilkes found the money for such a spread? By forming a company he could have raised it easily. But had Wilkes seen that? Had Wilkes the wit to realize that? Or had someone else pointed out the fact to him? Crowly, perhaps?

It might have been. Certainly the place had taken on new life since Crowly's advent.

Tune's thoughts moved again to that Crockett House shooting, to young Tim falling on the Crockett House porch. Stacey Wilkes, Tune thought, had been coached to that shooting. By someone who wanted young McClain put away.

Had the syndicate wanted McClain put away? Or had the someone been Crowly?

It was by no means certain that there

was a syndicate.

Who had knifed Teal?

And who had knifed Wilkes?

Had the same hand wielded the knife both times, or had someone willed to make it look that way?

The quickest way to get a range war brewing was to turn every outfit against its neighbor. While neighbor fought neighbor there was good chance for pickings.

Was Crowly the spider so busily weaving? Or was Jess but the hammer for a syndicate tool?

The man was in this thing someplace. Crowly knew about Tune who had come from San Saba. And Tune did not mean to forget that.

They cruised steadily along through the yellow flowered greasewood and, though he thought as he rode, Tune had an eye out for trouble. This was first class country for a man with a rifle.

The late afternoon drowsed on toward twilight and a dreaming stillness lay over this land, this tawny land stretching mile on mile to the misty blue of the faraway mountains.

There was little sound but the claybank's footfalls. An occasional lizard scampered over the trail, but mostly they rode through a vast kind of silence whose only company was the everlasting heat.

Just short of full dark the country's contour changed. The sun's molten copper was behind the far peaks and the greasewood flats had given way to a series of rolling slopes and cutbanks when Tune, coming leisurely out of a wash, caught the wink of a distant campfire, and a girl's voice suddenly, sharply said:

"Pull up!"

Tune stopped. Surprise pulled down his eye corners. He released them with a whimsical smile. "You sure get around, ma'am. You surely do."

It was the blue-eyed gitana.

She did not smile.

She wore levis now, denim pants stuffed into hand-tooled boots. She wore a man's woolen shirt. She looked surprised as he'd been.

"I want to thank you," Tune said, "for fetchin' my horse. It was an act of charity." He would have said more but she broke in swiftly.

"Where do you go to, prala?"

"A man always rides where fancy takes him. What do you do here, Blue Eyes?"

"But here!" she cried. "Why should you

ride here, prala?"

"Where a girl blocks a trail with a rifle, there is bound to be some reason for it."

"But I was not blocking the trail. I — I was hunting rabbits, prala. I heard your horse and I was frightened."

"What's to frighten a girl in this country?"

She shrugged slim shoulders and looked away from him.

It was Tune who finally broke the silence. "I don't believe I've heard your name. I am called Dakota. I shall always remember your goodness, chiquita —"

"Then go," she said quickly. "Go back to that yellow-haired one who sent you. There is nothing —"

"Nothing, querida?"

"My name is Panchita. No — nothing for you."

"There are sheep," Tune said. He could hear the sharp catch of her breath in the stillness.

"Have the sheep hurt you?"

"Sheep hurt the grass —"

"Not if they have a good shepherd with them."

"Cattle will not eat where sheep have been —"

"That is foolish! With my own eyes I have seen them eat!"

86

"Well, you've got to admit they spoil the water. Neither cattle nor horses will drink after sheep."

"So you would kill them! Is that your kindness, prala?"

"I am not a killer of sheep, Panchita."

"Then go back where you came from. Go back to that woman and tell her so!"

"But the cattle came first, chiquita. All this land is cattle country. It will remain so. You must turn your flocks and take them out of here."

She said nothing to that, and Tune said more sharply: "Do you hear, Panchita? You must get your sheep out of here."

"They are not mine. They belong to my uncle."

The wink of the distant campfire seemed brighter. It made the shadows seem deeper round them. Out of this darkness the girl spoke abruptly. "Come — come, prala. You shall speak with my uncle."

He saw the quick turn of her shoulders, heard the thud of her bootheels going off from him.

He walked the claybank after her; and a man's raised hail came down the wash and the girl's voice lifted, answering him.

They were not unprepared, he thought grimly. But if this girl belonged with these sheepmen, what business had taken her to Tucson? And how had she gotten there? And what had she been doing at Madam Belladine's brothel? And her language, too! That was not the talk of an ignorant gypsy.

She had the lure of mystery, this girl with the so-blue eyes.

Tune followed her into the sheep camp warily, searching the night for dark eyes behind rifles. But the night was too black for him to observe very much; the fire raised a wall of shadows which no human eye could pierce.

Tune watched the girl throw wood on the fire, fresh greasewood branches that burned like fat; and a voice came out of the shadows angrily. "Little fool! Would you have us all killed that you make such a brightness?"

"Come out of your hole, Tio Felix," she called (*Faylas* was the way she pronounced it). "I would have you talk with this caballero."

"These gringos — I cannot talk to them well. Is it about the sheep?"

"Yes. I would have you tell him about the sheep."

A little bent old man hobbled out of the shadows. He was like a little gnome in his soiled white cotton so pungent of sheep.

But his eyes were kindly. He did not look like a fighter. He did not look quite the kind to do much good in a range war. It made Tune wonder why the Seven Keys had picked him.

"Tell him about your sheep, Tio Felix."

"Tell me, rather," Tune said, "why you brought them here."

"I brought them here for the grass, your honor."

"Yes, of course. But who suggested you bring them here — the McClains?"

A brightness flared in the old man's eyes. They burned into Tune's like hot coals. "God forbid! Never would I do those robbers — but you would not understand, your honor. I have brought them back to the land of my fathers."

"That's all very well," Tune said, "but this is cow country."

The old man turned to the girl, his glance anxious. "What does he want with us? What does he want with my sheep? Why does he come here, Panchita?"

"He comes from the yellow-haired one," the girl said. "He says we must move the sheep out of here."

"No! No! No bueno por nada!" the old man cried. He shook his gnarled head; shook his stick in the air. He muttered a lot of swift Spanish.

Tune said: "The sheep cannot stay here, compadre. This is country for cows and the sheep are no bueno. You must move them, amigo."

Words tumbled out of the old man fiercely. Spanish words, too swift for Tune's catching.

Panchita looked at Tune. "He says —"

"Tell him to take it a little slower."

The old man mumbled it over again.

"He says —"

"Yes, I heard him. He is wrong. It makes no difference what the marshal told him. The marshal has nothing to do with this land. Tell him so. Tell him the marshal lied to him. This range belongs to the Clover Cross. He will have to move —"

"Never!" The old man glared at Tune angrily. "Never!"

"It makes no difference," Tune told the girl. "I am sorry about this, but the sheep must go. Marshal Safford was lying. His permission means nothing because he has no permission to give. You will have to get the sheep out of here —"

"Not a foot! Not a incha!" Felix shouted.

"Would it not be better to move them yourself than to have the cow boys move them for you?"

"But we can't!" the girl cried. "Tio Felix can't move them — he has no hombres — no man! They were frightened of Teal and have run away!"

"You could move them yourself if we gave you time —"

"It would take us too long. There are too many," she said.

"How much time would you need?"

The old man's eyes turned crafty. "Two weeks."

"Three days," Tune said, and Tio Felix cursed. He shook his stick at Tune angrily.

But Tune stood firm, for he knew he could not give them longer. "You will move the sheep in three days' time or the Clover Cross cow boys will come and shoot them."

Chapter 9

Tune felt no pride of that scene at the sheep camp. There was in him the feeling they had bested him some way. He could not put his finger on it, but the feeling stayed with him. There had been something — Take that girl waiting out on the trail with a rifle. That big, winking campfire with nobody round it but that one old man. And he had seen no sheep. Tune remembered that now.

He stopped his horse with an oath.

That was it! Where were the sheep? Where *were* the sheep?

They were not at that camp or he would have known it. He'd have heard them. Why, he had not even *smelled* any sheep, except the sheep smell on the old man's clothing.

That sly old man had made a fool of him! While he'd kept Tune by that campfire, talking, the sheep had been moving — moving deeper into Clover Cross!

A look came back to Tune then. The look he had seen in Lou Safford's eyes when he'd sprung that question about

Safford's money and sheep. Whether Lou had put money into sheep or not it was a pretty safe bet he was mixed in this deeper than any marshal's badge could have warranted.

Tune swung around in the saddle and threw a quick look at his backtrail. But there was a bend in the wash between him and the camp and he could not see the wink of its campfire.

Could there be any gain in further talk with old Felix?

Tune's shoulders moved impatiently. Then an odd thought caused him to swing from the saddle and lead his horse deep into the brush that so rankly grew beside this trail. He stood by the clay-bank's head and listened, and a thin unamused little smile crossed his lips and he clamped a hand to his mount's swelling nostrils.

The sound of a traveling horse came plainly.

Horse and rider flashed past like gray ghosts in the gloom and Tune took his grip front the claybank's face. That would be the old man, or it would be the girl riding by his order, gone to warn the men with the sheep or to give them some new change in direction.

Tune could find those sheep by tailing the rider.

But did he want to, right now?

He decided he did and was lifting a foot to swing into the saddle when muzzle flame burst from the night's crouched shadows. The claybank went up — went away back on its haunches; but Tune went up with him, went into the saddle. He flung himself forward and raked the big horse with his rowels. The horse lunged forward. Tune flung two shots toward the faded flash. He drove the horse all through that brush but there was no further firing and no sign of the firer.

He cut south for a ways, well clear of the trail, and a mile farther on returned to it with a gun held ready for trouble. And he had good reason to be glad of that. There was another horseman cutting in from the right, angling down from the brush stubbled slopes very carefully.

"Hold it!" Tune yelled, and heard a rattle of rocks as the downcoming man sat his horse on its haunches. The deeper black of the man's arched shoulders and hatted head vaguely showed against the lesser dark of the trail beyond.

"Kind of late for ridin', ain't it, friend?"

The man sat his horse stiffly still, unanswering. He must have guessed Tune had a gun trained on him, must have sensed in Tune's voice a degree of Tune's temper, for he kept his horse still, kept his hands still, also.

Then something about the set of those shoulders pulled up Tune's chin, and he said through tight lips. "Some of your habits stand in need of alterin'. For two cents, Ives, I'd take care of that for you."

Ives said: "You'd better get out of this while you're still able."

"Meanin' next time you might have better luck maybe? Don't count on it. Next time'll probably be the last chance you'll have at it."

Ives said nothing.

Tune said, "Maybe I'm figurin' this wrong, friend. I don't like a man that gets his duck from —"

"Why, you driftin' hound! When I come after *you* it won't be from no ambush!"

Tune could feel the man's glare. They sat their horses barely twenty feet apart, sat several moments without saying anything. Then Tampa said: "What you doin' rammin' round in the night?"

"Just what I was thinking of asking you."

"By God," Ives snarled, "I've got a *right* to be ridin'!"

"So have I," Tune said. "And I'll tell you something else, Mister Ives; I will ride where I please. Where I please and when I please. Remember it. If you want to play Mary's lamb with me —"

"Go on — keep swingin' it. I can wait," Tampa choked through the spleen in his voice. "What was you jawin' so long with that girl about?"

"So it *was* you!" Tune breathed softly. "Let me give you a little advice, Ives. When you make up your mind to shoot a man don't wait till it's dark and get into a thicket —"

"I'll guarantee you one thing," Ives shouted. "If I'd been gunnin' for you you'd been dead an' planted!"

"So maybe you was thinkin' to run a little bluff, eh?"

"You've had your warnin'. Make the most of it. Clover Cross is too small for you an' me both."

"I shall hate to see you packin' your warbag. But if I find you again with a gun pointed my way I shall see that the boys get some digging to do. Two can play at this flip-an'-shoot business, and when *I* play I play for keeps."

Tune watched Ives' shoulders fade away.

But not until Ives' sound had grown dim did Tune put away his pistol. Then he started thoughtfully home. He was still undecided about Ives Tampa when he rode into the moonless Clover Cross yard.

There was no one about, which might mean much or nothing. Tampa's horse wasn't in the corral. Tune unsaddled the claybank, hung his gear on the fence and leaned there, making a cigarette and smoking it, considering the various angles of this business. Were those sheep Lou Safford's? Or were they really Felix's?

After all, thus far, he had seen no sheep.

Leave them alone, ran the nursery rhyme, *and they'll come home, wagging their tails behind them.*

Well . . . maybe. At any rate, he knew too little about this range to go ramming around it in the middle of the night. The sheep would keep, some other things mightn't. Any moment now might bring a raid from Crowly. Any moment might bring trouble for the cattle; the ranch itself might be attacked, besieged to pen the crew inactive. But these were matters within Ives' province and had best, for the moment, be left there. Tune's was an outside job as outlined to him, his part to harry the enemy.

97

On sudden impulse he decided to ride.

He stubbed out his smoke on a pole of the fence, took his rope and went into the round enclosure. The horses rushed away from him but he settled his loop on a lineback dun and quickly, afterwards, saddled him.

He rode from the yard at an easy canter.

He would go to town. He would find Lou Safford. What good this might do him he did not know. It was a hunch and he would follow it. The danger to himself he discounted. If by seeing Safford he could save one life, could shorten this thing by only that much, he considered the risk well taken.

Lou was mixed up in this, and probably more than by his friendship with Crowly. Lou's self-seeking soul was a deal too canny to get mixed into anything simply for friendship. The marshal would be in this war for a profit and Tune must convince Lou the cards were against him.

He stepped up the dun's easy pace a little. The horse was fresh and a willing mover. The long and rangy look of him, his depth of girth and powerful muscles promised speed and a deal of stamina back of it. There was a very good chance they might need that bottom.

Oro Blanco's lights came before them presently, and it was then Tune wondered who had lost that button, the little red button hand carved from mesquite wood, he had found on the planking of Grankelmeir's stable.

Not the girl — surely not Panchita? Tio Felix, then? Was that little old man concerned in this?

Something recalled to Tune then the shot he had heard as he stood in this town with the marshal, Lou Safford, casually watching the crowd collect in front of Riske Quentin's — that sudden lone shot just ahead of Wilkes' pistol when Safford had cried out so bitterly: *"You see? Wherever you are, by God, there's trouble!"*

Lou seemed to be right about some things.

But who had fired that lone shot and at whom was it aimed?

It was plain to Tune all these things had meaning, some particular place in the web of evil that some dark spider was so slyly weaving. They were not random things, disjointed happenings whose trail led nowhere. They were parts of the sinister whole, tiny cogs, marshaled and aimed at this land's enslavement.

Tune's lips got a little tighter, and he

turned the dun toward Lou Safford's office that was back of the jail at the end of this street.

It was not Ives Tampa's intention to make the mistake big Teal had made. Spectacular plays and ultimatums had no part in Tampa's strategy. Both Larinda and Tune had counted him short when balanced in the light of things imminent and drastic. But Ives was full measure in his own odd fashion. He did not like trouble and could never invite it. For itself, that is. His stubborn nature saw no benefit in change. He liked old things. He liked all things to remain as he knew them. So long as he could he continued doggedly to shut his eyes to the things he could not countenance.

But shutting his eyes did not bring Teal back, nor could it undo the cold blooded killing of young McClain. That killing warned him of the things to come, finally opening his eyes to the danger of them.

If the spur were sharp Ives Tampa could act.

The spur was like a thorn in Ives' side as he whirled his horse and rode away from Tune. He distrusted the man and hated his calling. When he was sure he had passed

Tune's hearing he rode for town by the shortest trail.

He would as soon have trusted Jess Crowly or Wilkes as this drifter Larinda had hired for strayman. Ives had not spent forty-seven years in the saddle without picking up a few bits of wisdom. That wisdom told him Tune was a man on the dodge.

So his course was plain.

There is no man so set against sin as the once-erring man brought at last to the fold. By this same paradox, there was not a man in all Arizona so intolerant of outlaws as the Clover Cross ramrod, once an outlaw himself. "Who will live by the gun will die by it," he said; and it never occurred to Ives to doubt his judgments.

Larinda he regarded as both foolish and headstrong. No girl was fitted to run a ranch anyway. Running a ranch was entirely a man's work. Ives realized now they would have to fight for Clover Cross. He could understand the desire which had prompted Larinda to hire this gun fighter. Desire for revenge was a common failing, and in this instance desire and necessity rode the same bronc. But Ives could not understand the girl's blindness. What folly! What madness! To pick a Seven Keys man

101

to fight the Seven Keys!

It was Ives' intention to rectify this blunder. If there were sheep on Clover Cross the sheep could wait. As Tampa saw it, getting rid of Tune was a heap more important than shoving a bunch of sheep back in the greasewood. Sheep he could manage. Nobody could manage a goddam outlaw!

Ives had known Safford casually for several months. He was not acquainted with the marshal's politics. His knowledge of Lou went no deeper than a few good drinks exchanged at the bar. He had always found Lou impeccably courteous, an open-minded gentleman comfortably inclined toward preserving law and order. Ives could not think how Tune had escaped Lou. He figured Seven Keys trickery must have had some large part in it. That Seven Keys outfit was a nest of snakes.

Ives expected the marshal would feel pretty happy over the prospect of taking Tune back into custody.

In the marshal's office Lou Safford was uncomfortably fiddling with a penknife and trying to look engrossed with the business. Three pairs of uncharitable eyes were on him and apprehensive shivers were playing with his spine. There was no use making up tales to account for it; he had let that gun fighter get clear away from him. Tune had done what Lou had hoped he would do, only in Lou's intentions Tune had not got away. Lou was right now wishing he had never heard of Tune.

He did not like the way Crowly was eying him. He did not like the way any of them were. This pair with Jess were not town drifters; they were tough hired guns — this Loma Jack packed two.

Loma Jack's cold sneer set Lou's teeth on edge.

And Cibecue, with his mismatched eyes and twisted foot had always made Lou feel uneasy. Loma Jack never trusted anyone, but a man couldn't tell what that Cibecue was thinking. Lou had sometimes wondered if he thought at all.

He took a slanchways glance at these fellows.

The cast of their features did not calm him any. "You yeller-bellied rat," the reedy Cibecue snarled, "I've a notion t' bash your face in!"

"Wait!" Loma Jack murmured softly.

Jess Crowly's mouth shaped a civilized smile. "Guess you played into a little tough luck, Lou. Might have happened to any of us, but the boys is naturally feelin' put out a bit. They're kind of figurin' what you done was mostly deliberate. But thet ain't my notion. I don't think you're thet kind of a felleh. I'm allowin' you'd like mighty well to prove it. Fact is," Jess said, "I come by to give you a chance t' prove it."

With his backbone feeling like red ants were at it, Lou made the try to look pleased with the prospect. But it seemed like his tongue had swelled up and petrified. He couldn't get out the word of thanks that looked called for. He couldn't, right then, say anything.

But Crowly didn't seem to notice.

Crowly went on urbanely: "Yep. I'm figurin' to give you a right good chance, Lou. I know how it is with this gun packin' business. The breaks sometimes go ag'in' you. What I got in mind now don't call fo' much luck — jest a eve'yday piece o' routine, as you might say. It's a chore I could give to Jack, heah, or Cibecue. But I want you should hev yo' chance to convince them. I wan—" Crowly smiled. "I want you should get rid of Ives Tampa fo' me."

"Ives Tampa!" cried Lou. "Why Tampa, for God's sake?"

"Because thet gel has made Tampa range boss. With Tampa gone Tune will be her top screw, an' with Tune roddin' Cloveh Cross we don't need t' figure the plays so damn ca'ful. This Tune is a flip-an'-shoot killer an' we can plaster his outfit with the same kind of rep."

Lou Safford looked round him uneasily.

"We will see that it does," Loma Jack smiled thinly.

Crowly said, "This will be duck soup fo' a man of yo' talents, Lou. Jest rid us of Tampa — that's all we ask, Lou. With Tampa out of the way the gel will make Tune her boss — bound to. Then we'll pull a few things an' git you made sheriff."

"But," Lou said nervously, "I still don't see how that's going to help much."

"Why," Jess smiled, "we make Cloveh Cross look like a outlaw hideout. Then we ride in an' smash it. That's simple, ain't it? We're tryin' to clean up the country — tryin' t' make it safe fo' the women an' kids."

"An' we'll do it, too," Loma Jack grinned sourly.

"But what about these other outfits —"

"They needn't git in yo' hair," Crowly told him. "I got deals on the fire with most of 'em anyway. Them I ain't can be scared out easy. Let 'em heah what's happened to

105

Cloveh Cross. They'll be rollin' their cotton in a hurry."

Lou dabbed several times at the sweat that was on him. The sweat kept coming. It was colder than hell with the blower off.

Lou said, "It seems to me we're kind of crowdin' things. What's the rush? It looks —"

"The only looks you need to be botherin' about is the looks of Ives Tampa," Loma Jack said bluntly.

Crowly considered Lou tolerantly. "That's right, Lou. That's all you got to worry about. And I'll give you some help. I'll give you Cibecue here for a deputy."

"I don't need no deputy —"

"You're goin' to hev one, anyway."

Crowly's smile worked on Lou like a sunstroke. He sank back in his chair like an old, old man.

Chapter 10

Could Lou Safford have known whom this night would bring riding he would have done quite a number of things differently. He would have stage-set the scene and had things watchfully ready like a whole string of firecrackers tied to one fuse. For Lou was a man who liked all the trimmings and he was a man, above all, who liked things safe. This was not so attributable to any fear bred in him as it was to the educated habits of his calling. A professional gambler likes the odds in his favor, and Lou had been professional all of his life.

But he had no means of foreseeing the future. After Crowly had left with his gun-weighted bravos Lou slouched moodily a considerable while in his chair. It was all the fault of that damned Dakota. Lou had known the moment he had seen Tune that the nice Old Lady was going to fold up her tent. He should have taken his hunch then and quit this place; he should have gone as far as a good horse could take him. He should have gone at once.

Lou was not afraid of this Dakota Tune. He was not afraid of him in any physical sense. It was psychologically Tune had Lou whipped.

Lou had thought when he saw Tune he had ought to get out of this, and he was asking himself if that were not still a good notion when he heard the rumor of an approaching rider. The horse came along and stopped at Lou's tie rack.

Saddle leather creaked. A boot thumped ground. A second boot followed and came up the steps with a measured tread and spur sound scraped the planks of the porch.

Lou pulled the desk's top drawer a little open.

He was facing the door when Ives Tampa walked in, and the look of his gambler's cheeks showed nothing. His nod was courteous, and he said with the tone he reserved for this man, "How are you, Ives? A fine evening, isn't it."

Tampa grunted. He brought his stoop-shouldered shape inside and closed Lou's door and stood a moment shaping his thoughts.

"Drag up a chair and sit down," Lou said affably. "How's the cow business these days? How's Miz McClain? I can't tell you how shocked I was about that killing. I'd have arrested Wilkes if that gun fighter, Tune —"

"I came in to see you about Tune, Lou. He's out at the ranch — the girl's hired him," Ives scowled.

Safford brought up his look with a show of interest. He flexed his lean fingers thoughtfully. "He's out at Clover Cross, you mean?"

There was a lean, hating look in the depths of Ives' eyes.

"Yeah, I figured you might like to know."

Behind his gambler's face Safford's thoughts moved swiftly. His fingers drummed a lazy rhythm. He wondered how much this gaunt Tampa knew. The man had not ridden in just to do Lou a favor. What *had* he come in for? In fear lest Tune cut him out of a job? Was that feeling strong enough for Seven Keys to use? Would there be anything in this for Lou Safford personally?

Lou said, "You ain't figuring on hunting new pasture, are you?"

"What put that fool idea in your head?"

Lou Safford shrugged. "Miz McClain shouldn't have put that outlaw on. Hate to see that girl . . ." Safford shook his head.

109

"Two wrongs never made a right in this world —"

Tampa said impatiently: "You better git you a posse an' git out here after him. While you're swingin' your jaw —"

"Hell!" Safford said. "I've no authority outside this town."

Tampa's eyes turned black. "You ain't goin' to let that stop you, are you?"

"Well, hardly," Lou smiled. "Makes a difference in how I go at it, though. I've got to think this out. You going to be here a spell?"

"I wasn't figuring to be. If you're wantin' that feller you better be gettin' on out there."

Lou said: "I'll get —" and, like that, quit talking. He was froze, half turned on the edge of his chair, when the door banged open and the man with the mismatched eyes limped in.

Irritation lifted Lou's shoulders.

"Cibecue," he said in a held-down voice, "try knocking some time. You will find it good practice. *Now what do you want?*"

Cibecue brought his look off Ives. "You fergot t' give me my tin," he leered. "What kinda deppity would I be with no badge?" His unfocused glance skittered back to Ives. "Who's this?"

110

Lou opened another drawer and tossed the gun man a nickeled star. "There you are. Close the door on your way out, will you?"

Cibecue's vacant laugh rattled forth. "I ain't gone yet. Who *is* this feller — ain't Ives Tampa, is he?"

Ives Tampa snarled: "Yes! Now git the hell out of here!"

Cibecue's half-witted face gleamed with pleasure. He scrubbed a hand on his dirty trousers. "Ives Tampa?" he said, limping over to Ives. "I'm right proud to know you! Say — what's that you got all over your hat?"

Ives snatched off his hat and Cibecue thumped Ives' head with a pistol.

Ives dropped down on the floor without argument.

Cibecue's mismatched eyes flicked to Lou. "What you been waitin' for? What do you want I should do with him now?"

Lou said drily: "I sure as hell don't want him left here."

He looked at his hands and fixed his fingers. "Get him on a horse and take him out to the ranch."

"Take him out to the Clover Cross?"

"Hardly. Take him out to Seven Keys. I'll tell Jess —"

111

"Jess ain't in town no more."

"Where is he?"

Cibecue shrugged. "Hell! He don't tell me."

"Never mind. You take Tampa out to the ranch — and don't be seen doing it. I'll get hold of Jess someway. I've got an idea — Do you want any help getting him onto his horse?"

"Don't you worry about me."

Lou picked up his hat. He smoothed down its knap with a careful elbow and, while Cibecue watched with a sneer on his face, set it jauntily atop his corn-yellow curls. He buttoned his coat and picked up his gloves.

"You look like a goddam dude!" growled Cibecue, and spat on his hands and heaved Tampa's limp shape across his shoulder.

Lou nodded. "I'll still be looking like one long after you're planted."

Tune, well knowing the risk he ran, stepped into Lou's office and found it empty. But the lamp in its bracket on the wall still burned, so he thought it unlikely Lou would be away long.

"Might as well wait," he thought, closing the door. "Probably down to Riske Quentin's."

He put his shoulders against the wall and leaned there awhile and frowned at the windows. He regretted that Lou had not drawn the shades. It would not be smart for him to draw them himself. Someone might see him or Lou, when he came, might notice. Better stay where he was, just inside the door. Lou would probably come in and head straight for his desk. At any rate, this way, Lou wouldn't see him till he got clear inside.

He wouldn't see Tune's horse for Tune had left the dun in a clump of brush at the edge of town. He felt reasonably certain he had arrived here unheralded.

He got to wondering about that blue-eyed gitana. She didn't look much like the old man, he thought. She didn't seem to have much in common with him, either. Maybe it was the sheep that bound them together. She used a pretty good brand of Spanish for a gypsy. He was aware of an increasing interest in her. A fellow wouldn't have to exert much effort to get himself interested in a girl like her. Yet it was odd, he thought, how well he remembered her, each trick and shading of her mobile features. He could only remember the yellow-haired girl as she'd been on the porch when Wilkes shot her brother.

He was like that, considering, his eyes roving around, when abruptly his glance sharpened into grim focus.

There was a battered old hat tumbled under the desk. A hat with a faded tiger-snake band. It had not been placed there of deliberate intent; it looked to have rolled there, to have been forgotten.

Tune knew that hat. It belonged to Ives Tampa.

Unthinkingly Tune stepped away from the wall.

He was bending to pick up Ives' hat and examine it when a girl's scream loudly sheared through the night and a window, behind him, broke into fragments as a gun beat up wild echoes in the street.

Chapter 11

There are some kinds of men who naturally gravitate toward women and Birch Alder, the Clover Cross bronc peeler, was of this persuasion. Obviously looks have little to do with it for Birch was a heavy handed, rough sort of man with a blue-black jaw and eyes frankly cast on the gimlet pattern. A cud of tobacco usually bulged his cheek and there was a knife scar over his opposite eye, giving his look at the world a kind of uncaring truculence. A good many women, despite this, had built fond dreams around Birch Alder.

According to Birch the world owed him plenty and he was out to get it any way he could. He was a man who had worked for many outfits and at each place, or within its vicinity, he had always managed to find him a woman. He preferred them young and with fire in their veins, but any kind would do if it had to. "Hell! It's only their names that's different," he'd say, and be off with a wink to find him another.

An old dog can be taught new tricks yet

its essential character remains unchanged. It was that way with Birch.

After signing on with Teal to ride rough string Birch had one day seen a certain look he knew in the eyes of Larinda McClain. She was on the top rail in her levis, watching him.

A wink was as good as a nod to Birch.

With his own eye, as ever, strictly on the main chance, he had taken himself right in hand from that moment. He knocked the rougher edges off the worst of his manners and took to aiming his expectorations where they showed least later. He even gave up the habit when Larinda was around him. He shaved more frequently, talked less about women.

Clover Cross was a damned fine ranch.

Birch believed in signs when the signs were favorable, and he found plenty of signs he was on the right track. Take that time she had picked him out of the bunch to go with her to look at cows in Tubac. Or that more recent time, not a week gone by, when she'd taken him with her to inspect the watershed. Why, he'd even had her right up against him!

She might be the boss but she was plenty human!

It was, therefore, with considerable of a

shock that, right after Teal's death, he found she'd made Tampa range boss. It was a dirty damned trick and Birch was not forgetting it! Why, that damned old Tampa was old enough to be her grandpaw!

Birch fumed and smouldered with enranged resentment. What kind of a woman was she? Kiss a man and make another guy foreman! Why, she hadn't no more ethics than a goddam jackrabbit!

Birch commenced to look over some things in his mind. There was a heap of things could happen to a man when he took to riding nightherd in this country. Lots of guys had fell over cliffs — there was such a thing as justice, by God!

While he was deciding how best he might aid it, Larinda sent for him up at the house.

Full dark had fallen and she had the lamps lit. He found her standing before a little piece of mirror propped up on the mantel. Birch stared at her, startled. She was doing up her hair and taking both hands to it.

Birch found it hard to keep his mind on justice. She hadn't much on underneath that wrapper.

There was times, Birch decided, when a

coal-oil lamp could be a real satisfaction.

Without turning, Larinda asked through the pins in her mouth, "Where's Ives and that new fellow?"

"What you wantin' them for?"

"If it concerns you, Birch, you will probably be told when the time is right for it."

Birch liked neither the words nor the smile with which, like an afterthought she garnished them. All the black thoughts in him began to boil up and he said with the words gritted out through his teeth:

"So it's Birch the Hired Hand you're talkin' to now, eh?"

The tone of his voice brought her eyes around to him. She eyed him a moment across her shoulder. Then her red lips curved in that warm kind of smile and he felt desire climbing out of the ashes. He cursed, and a downswinging blow of his hand thumped the table. "By God," he cried, "can't you never stay put!"

She laughed at him then and went back to her primping.

Birch, still scowling, blackly watched the way of the lamp with her contours.

"Are they still around?"

"Them rannies? I dunno," Birch growled like it strangled him.

"And Crispin's out with the cattle . . .

118

Where's Wimpy Gilman?"

"He's around someplace — I see him awhile ago fixin' his saddle." Birch considered her more carefully. "What's up? What you wantin' that little wart fer?"

"How do you feel about taking a ride, Birch?"

Birch perked up. "I allus feel like ridin' — with you."

She swung away from the mirror then, swung round to face him. She had her hair up now. Shimmering braids of gold, like a halo. She grinned. "Not *that* kind of ride." She got a pair of levis and a man's rough shirt from the corner closet, and Birch Alder's thoughts put a shine in his eyes.

Larinda saw that look and she smiled a little and Birch came across the floor tumultuously. But she put both hands up against him, and holding him that way let him kiss her. Just once. Then she pushed him back. "Later," she said. "Later Birch — later. We haven't time now. The Seven Keys' payroll is on that stage from Ajo. We'll take Gilman — Hurry! Catch up the horses while I get into these clothes."

Chapter 12

Jess Crowly, a long while back, had used to claim he hailed from El Paso — and he might have done it, but not originally. As a matter of fact, Jess' mother had borne him on the opposite side of the River in an eight-by-ten mud shack of a house that belonged to a one-eyed Indio. The place didn't have any windows, and the only door was a tow sack strip that didn't come down to below a man's knees, and the Old Man had killed three Rurales through it when they'd come dropping around for a chat with Jess' mother. It was right after this Jess hailed from The Pass.

The Señora Crowly had been a mighty fashionable looking woman in her day; right many a guitar had been plunked by her window and she had been trothed by fond parents to a man of fine family, old Jesus Juan Bravo y Vandalera, the Alcalde of Juarez. But these plans had gone agley someway. Just prior to the ceremony Jess' mother had chanced to be passing the jailhouse and glimpsed the rogue face of Kane

Crowly grinning back at her.

Ah, those were the days!

Red heeled slippers and caballero spurs. Lips gay with laughter. Sweet hours of madness when blood was hot and quick to run and the way of a maid needed no explaining. Those were the days! Moonlight and stars through the breeze-swayed trees. Writhing bodies and the sharp click of castanets. Frijoles y cuchillos. José Cuervo in a gleaming glass and wild cries winging through the hoof-torn night when a man's life hinged on the speed of his horse and only the bold had their way with a maid.

But life with Kane Crowly proved a little too fast. Few were the hearts that could stand the pace. Dona Ysabel died stripped of her youth and stripped of beauty. Speed was the measure of an outlaw's passion and speed, the begetter, packs its own wild challenge and the time always comes when the pistol drops from the paralyzed hand; and so it was with Kane Crowly one night. From that hour on it was young Jess Crowly against the world.

He was only a kid, but the border blood burned hot in his veins and he was swift to learn the ways of the land. No humdrum honest life for Jess! He preferred to die

121

with his boots on, and said so. He took to the gun and, with his agile wits and ready hand, took the top of the Wanted list in no time. Banks and stages were his special dish; then he heard of the James boys, the Youngers and Ketchum, and decided he could tame the Iron Horse, too. He stopped one close to Pecos one night; stopped a second not far from Shakespeare. Then he took his bunch to the Cherokee Strip and Doolin's gang wiped Jess' bunch plumb out.

Jess went back to Texas a wiser man, but not near as wise as he figured he was. The Border Patrol caught Jess one night with a bunch of wet cattle coming out of the River on the U.S. side, and the next few years he took a course in rock breaking. At the State's expense.

But all things pass if you can wait long enough. Jess had little choice in the matter. When they let him out he was a reformed character. He had not changed a great deal in appearance; he was the same dark, short and broad fellow he had been — more quiet, perhaps, more given to thinking and more controlled of temper. It was all in his head, but the boy they had set to breaking up rocks walked out of the jailhouse a man full grown. A man fundamentally different as night from day; a man gone wrong to his rotten core. A man haunted and hounded by the things in his mind, by the repressions of those years and by the imagined taint they had put upon him.

The inherited tendencies were also there, much strengthened — nurtured and intensified by those years on the rockpile, grown and bloated by those years of brooding that only a prisoned man can so nourish. Two things only were gone from his heritage — love of nature and the gift of laughter. Those were gone, burnt out in the ashes of those cooped-up years. The wind and the stars, the vast silence of deserts, the majesty of mountains held neither meaning nor interest for Jess. Not for him the lonely campfire or the way of a moon playing through white clouds. Not even the feel of a good bronc's barrel between his legs could bring any answering thrill to this man he was become. Recklessness and that wild fierce temper still rode with Jess, but caution held a leash on them now, and they were fused by subtlety, polished by craft. His was the same atavistic nature, but sharply honed now by perception, by the thoughts engendered of past experience.

Jess Crowly knew what he wanted now.

He wanted power and he knew how to get it.

He had tried out his talents and the knowledge of power was yeasty in him. All things come to the man who can wait. Every man gets what he wants if there is enough determination in him to keep after it. What you get, Jess believed, is a matter of your own intensity, the intensity of your desire and the measure of your endurance. Given bottom and will a man can have everything. This was Crowly's creed, the refined result of observation and experience.

After the warden had said goodbye to him Jess had covered a deal of territory, just drifting and watching with his ear to the ground. San Saba had presented Jess with a set-up ripe for his talent. A young rancher named Tune was hip deep in trouble. The bone of contention was a vast spread of grasslands Tune's father had held under lease and developed. The elder Tune had had vision. He had improved the property with buildings and fences; irritation and industry had done away with the native growths until today the Tune range was an evergreen series of lush meadows knee-deep in the nourishment of succulent fodders. It would feed well upwards of six thousand cattle. A good fat lease, just what Jess was hunting for.

He had studied Tune's various envious neighbors, seeking their weaknesses, discovering their virtues. The inroads of prowling cinch-ring experts had reduced young Tune to a minimum of cash. His sole negotiable assets were four-footed ones, line-bred horses and those fine white-faced cattle he'd been building up with the aid of four imported registered bulls. The lease money payment date had been extended and was now again due when Jess rode into San Saba one morning.

The outfit back of Tune's rustling troubles was a syndicate spread which operated under the somewhat ambiguous title of the Lone Star Land & Cattle Combine. They were after Tune's lease. They would have to pay for his improvements, of course, but they were well-heeled with capital and eager to do so — if they couldn't get hold of the place any other way. Tune was not well liked, he was too desperately envied. He was considered an upstart by those less fortunate.

Jess looked around. He found the man with the most influence in Tune's community was one Blackwell Stokes, the High

Commissioner.

Jess, in the guise of an out-of-state cattleman, cultivated Stokes with care and circumspection. He suspected Stokes of the common hunger and he subsequently found his suspicions well founded. Like the syndicate outfit, the admirable Stokes was after Tune's lease. Stokes was the town's most solid citizen, an institution almost, a pillar of the Church. Not only was Stokes High Commissioner, he was also president of the local bank. A very choice state of affairs, Crowly thought, and proceeded to fit himself into things.

It seemed the greatest obstacle to Stokes' ambition was the Lone Star Land & Cattle Combine. It was Jess who ironed out that angle for him. Jess laughed every time he thought of that business.

Tune, finding himself increasingly short, became increasingly unlikely to scrape up enough money to renew his lease. Tune consulted his friend, Banker Stokes, and inquired if there were any way in which he could save his stake. Why certainly, Stokes said, the bank would advance the money. Naturally Tune would have to assign his lease-hold over to Stokes as security, and the loan, unfortunately, could not be extended over a longer period than ninety days. That was all right, Tune said. He could still gather up and market sufficient good beef in that time to more than pay off this obligation.

So, with the lease money due by noon on the morrow, Tune had come into the bank next evening, just before closing time, and completed the deal. Stokes had given him the money, a substantial sum, in hundred dollar bills. Jess, posted outside, had watched Tune putting the money away. When Tune left the bank Jess followed him.

Jess idled in an adjacent doorway while Tune ate supper in a nearby hash house and dawdled over the evening paper. It was almost dark when Tune finished and left and, as Stokes and Jess had figured he would, stopped in at the Grubstake Saloon.

Almost any man would with his worries lifted suddenly as Tune's had been.

The Grubstake was a cowtown place, typical of its kind. Some folks called it the Carlton House Bar because it stood next door to that hostelry and the hotel had no bar of its own. There was nothing pretentious about it. It held a pretty fair crowd that evening and the games already were creating excitement for this was a Saturday night in San Saba and payday for many of the roundabout ranches. Jess, looking in through the batwings, saw Tom Curry, the sheriff, alongside the bar not far from Tune's elbow.

A sagebrush orchestra — one fiddler and a swarthy Mexican strumming a guitar — was furnishing the noise and the light was furnished by three hanging lamps just over the bar.

Jess took a good look over his shoulder then whipped out his pistol and fired four times.

Pandemonium filled that place on the instant.

The hanging lamps came down with a crash, and through the murk Jess wove like a cat. Shouts and oaths made a battering din while Jess slugged at Tune through that wild press of bodies and abruptly shied off with a hand round Tune's wallet. He got off with it, too; and when the bartender got his candle lit there was Tom Curry sprawled dead on the floor and Tune crouched over him with a smoking pistol.

"Goddam sheriff killer!"

It was Jess cried that from outside the door, but the crowd took it up and Tune left by a window.

Tune had not seen Jess — did not

know Jess from Adam.

Jess trailed him over to the banker's house where Tune went to see Stokes in Stokes' capacity as Commissioner. Stokes appeared sympathetic. He listened gravely while Tune excitedly told what had happened. How he'd been in the Grubstake getting a drink when some damn fool had up and shot the lights out. In the ensuing darkness and resultant confusion, someone had snatched Tune's wallet; Tune had fired, hoping to drop the man. When the bartender's candle had brought things back into focus Tom Curry, with a hand thrust into his coatfront, lay dead on the floor.

Stokes' hand had gone worriedly through his white hair. He had finally, gloomily, shaken his head. "I'm sorry, Tune. This has gone too far. Neither repentance nor innocence can reshuffle the cards. The man is dead — you cannot change that. You cannot escape your connection with it. There are powerful factions at work in the land . . ."

Stokes had sighed like the world's whole weight was on him.

"I hate mighty bad to say this to you, son, but it looks like you had better travel. For awhile, anyway. This town is too riled to split hairs right now. You'd better dig for the tules and stay hid for a spell. That was probably a frame-up to get Tom Curry — no telling who killed him; we may never know. The man had powerful enemies. But when the authorities get to the bottom of this you will doubtless be cleared and can come back to your own again. I'll take care of your lease . . ."

Jess gave him that — Stokes had certainly intended to.

It was a slick piece of work all around, and none of it slicker than the part Stokes wasn't aware, of the part of the business that was yet to come. Jess Crowly's big part.

With Tune gone larruping off into hiding Stokes had made haste to protect Stokes' interest. He paid the annual rent on the lease. He put a big crew of riders armed with guns on the place, for he held bona-fide notes on the most of Tune's cattle and had no wish to be done out of them. He allowed Jess Crowly to keep the money Jess had got from Tune's wallet, hinting there'd be more ere the deal was finished.

That was Crowly's notion, also.

It was Jess who had seen the real chance in this business. What a fool Stokes would be, he had pointed out, to keep that lease and bring the syndicate down on him. That lease, Jess declared, was a hot potato. There might always be trouble over that damned lease — hadn't the syndicate mighty near ruined Tune to get it? Did Stokes think they would stop because the lease had changed hands? That L.S.L. & C.C. crowd wouldn't stop at anything. So why not make a deal with them? Why not sell them the place and to hell with them?

"Don't forgit," Jess said, "you still got Tune t' consider. He ain't goin' to like this a little bit. The guy holdin' this lease is like t' stop a few bullets!"

"If you'd gunned the fool according to plan —"

"Plans," Jess said, "is subjeck t' human limitations. I done what I could, but I ain't no cat — I can't see in the dark no better'n the next guy! Could I guess Curry was goin' t' jump in front of him?"

Stokes had muttered but he'd finally come around. The syndicate could afford to pay well for that lease. But Stokes had himself been having some trouble with them — Jess knew this, he had himself engineered it. Stokes said he doubted if they'd do business with him.

"I'll take care o' that," Jess told him. "You leave it t' me. I can deal with those tough guys. I know all about 'em. Will fifty thousan' take care o' you?"

"How much are *you* thinking to pull down out of it?"

"I'll git mine from you after the deal's finished. Name yo' price an' I'll see what I can do fo' you."

So, while Jess was carrying on negotiations, Stokes had got busy on the law end of things. He took the business to court and sued to foreclose on the note the outlawed Tune had given him, and to have the court transfer the lease which Tune had put up as security for the note, and to have it set over into his, Stokes', name. By the time this was accomplished Jess had a deal lined up with the syndicate.

"But they don't want t' pay mo' than fo'ty thousan'," Jess said, looking to see how Stokes would take it.

"They'll pay fifty thousand or I'll peddle it elsewhere — what do they take me for?" Stokes demanded. "There's plenty outfits round here would like that lease. And tell them I want the money in War Bonds — I don't want none of that 'bearer' stuff. I want Civil War Bonds — Series X."

Jess scratched his head like this was all above him. He said: "They ain't goin' t' like it, Blackwell. Thet's a touchy bunch —

meaner than gar soup. They been figurin'
to give you a check —"

"They can figure again. I want Civil War
Bonds! They'll do this *my* way — or someone else will! That lease won't go begging
for fifty thousand!"

So Jess rode back to the syndicate again,
and the L.S.L. & C.C. finally agreed to
Stokes' terms; and that was how Jess had
come to leave Texas.

Stokes made out the papers and called in
some clerks to witness his signature. "Here
you are," he told Jess, folding them into an
envelope. "Tell those highbinders to get
those bonds in the mail right away; you
stay right with them and be damned sure
they do. Don't give them these papers —
Hold on! Wait, let me think."

Stokes had sat there scowling at his desk
for a moment. Then he'd looked up at Jess
and nodded, like he was putting the go-
ahead sign on his thinking. "Guess you'd
better fetch those bonds back yourself;
those crooks might stick up the stage, or
something. A bunch like that will stoop to
anything."

"Yeah, they're salty all right," Jess
grinned at him. "But I'll watch 'em! Er . . .
How much you figurin' my time's been
worth to you?"

Stokes looked at Jess from under his eyebrows. "I never forget my friends," he said solemnly. "You got five thousand dollars coming the minute you put those bonds in my hand."

That was the way Stokes had got Jess figured; and it kind of riled up Jess' bowels that anyone should take him for such a dumb cluck.

He must have showed his face pretty satisfied though, because Stokes kind of sniffed and took his look off Jess and commenced rattling papers the way bankers do when they've used up time beyond a customer's value. Jess halfway looked for him to dust off the seat just so quick as Jess got his bottom out of it. But that was all right with Jess. He was being well paid to take insults.

He picked up the envelope and put on his hat. *"Al garanon no le inporta lo que el patrio dija de el,"* he murmured, and Stokes jerked a nod at him absently, his mind gone already to another transaction.

That was the last Jess had seen of him. He delivered the papers, got the bonds from the syndicate and took the next train out of Texas. Blackwell Stokes, he considered, was a plain damn fool.

Leaving the Marshal's office, Crowly

took his two gun men down to Riske Quentin's and bought them a drink; then he gave them instructions and took his departure.

For just a bit things had had Jess rattled, the way this thing was developing. But it was all right now. The end was inevitable. With Tampa out of the way, the girl, if she would not play along with Jess, was bound to give Tune Tampa's job. And that was all Jess asked for. Let her make Tune boss and Jess would get Lou Safford made sheriff and the rest could be left up to Safford's posses. Not even Safford's cold feet could make any ultimate difference then, for Jess meant to pick the posse men himself and he would pick the kind who would do as he told them.

The world, Jess thought, was filled with damned fools.

Chapter 13

Blackwell Stokes, the San Saba banker and county commissioner, was a hypocrite and a pernicious rascal and, under his country gentleman guise, he was one other thing — a disliker of children. He would not have them around. They disrupted the ordered run of his thoughts. They took his mind off more profitable matters. He disliked the sticky feel of their fingers, their shouts and shrill voices, their bickering and whining. Nonetheless, in the early days of his marriage, he had tried for a son to carry on his business. Childbirth had cost him the life of his wife, and the child she bore him was one without tassel — a sniveling, blubbering brat of a girl which he shipped off at once to the care of relatives. This had solved her problem for awhile until divorce had forced him to find other caretakers. He never spoke of her, never wrote to inquire of her welfare; his checks were regular and the full extent of his interest in her.

After eight years of being farmed out, she was placed in a convent at Corpus

Christi. There she remained in the sheltered obscurity of eight other years. On her fourteenth birthday Blackwell Stokes came to see her and was completely dumbfounded by her charm and beauty. He at once gave thought to her possible marriage and thought over the names of possible husbands. He decided he would have her come home for a bit. He inquired if she might come home for the holidays. Mother Superior thought it quite possible if Mr. Stokes would provide suitable escort.

It was thus arranged, and for a handful of days in her fifteenth year Mary Jacqueline Stokes visited the home of her father. She found everything strange and exciting. San Saba of those days was a rough community of crude boardwalks and false-fronted buildings that had been slapped up of planks and tarpaper. It had much quaint charm to delight the child's vast energy and interest; but Stokes had had no time to waste on such foolery. He had not brought her this long way from Corpus to spend his time in showing her the town; he had brought her here that the town might see *her* — or such of the town as he deemed advantageous. Collectively he held his neighbors in low esteem, regarding them privately as uncouth backwoodsmen descended from the illicit unions of ruffians and hurdy girls; his daughter was not for any such trash. She was bait for cash balances and met only the most affluent of the bank's clientele, three wrinkled old rakes whose accounts ran into the six-figures bracket and whose lecherous looks made the girl blush hotly. She disliked particularly the tall skinny one with the parfleche face whose continual grin showed repulsive rows of decaying teeth and whose breath was a blast beyond endurance.

So when, one summer's evening in her sixteenth year, Sister Teresa unhappily disclosed her father's plan to her, Mary Jacqueline's voice rose in whole-souled rebellion.

"But I don't *wish* to marry that awful old man — I don't wish to marry *anyone!*" ...

"Hush, child," the good Sister admonished. "These are matters for older heads — what could one so young know of marriage! Such matters are best left to one's parents; besides, it is the custom. The child's duty is obedience to family. You will find it will all work out very well. Parents consider these things in the light of experience. Your father is a prominent man in his community, he would not make other than suitable plans —"

"But —"

"Hush, child. You must have faith. Your father tells us it will be a fine match —"

"With that old goblin!" Mary Jacqueline wailed. "Why, he's old enough to be my great grandfather! He has bleeding gums and mossy teeth — his eyes are like black spiders, Sister!"

Mary Jacqueline felt she must talk with her father. If she could explain her feeling she felt sure her father would not insist on this marriage. Arranged futures might be the custom, but at least let the arrangement include a man more personable. She felt sure she could make her father understand. She must go to him at once!

She went with the money he had given her for Christmas; stole away from the convent, crept away like a furtive thief in the night.

It was also night when she arrived in San Saba, night and full dark with the town gaily lit by saloon-front torches and kerosene lanterns. Her father's house showed a lamp in the study. The door was unlocked and she let herself in quietly, lest she disturb her father's housekeeper, a timid old soul who probably needed her sleep.

The girl knew her way from previous

visits and, thinking how delighted Stokes would be to see her, went at once to his study and opened the door.

He had company that night, a short and broad man with a dark-burnt face and burly shoulders whose muscles showed ropelike through his pongee shirt. This man grinned disagreeably as her father talked. Several times he nodded and rubbed at his cheek, but always his mouth showed that dark sly smile.

Her father seemed to be outlining some projected program concerned with some rancher he contemptuously referred to as 'that fool Tune.' So engrossed were the pair with developing their plans they failed utterly to notice the wide-eyed girl in the doorway.

Her words of greeting died away unspoken. She stood very tense and straight visioning the things her father was unfolding. She would have cried out against them but no words would come; she would have fled undiscovered but the cold calculations of their villainy froze her, anchoring her there as with chains of steel.

She remained and heard, repelled yet fascinated as a bird is fascinated by the look of a snake, by the snake's sinuous body, by its weaving head. It was all too monstrous, too unreal — incredible. Yet there they sat, her father and that man, nodding and smiling like two old friends talking over old times.

She found it revolting, nauseous; it someway made her feel unclean. Yet she stood there, listening, unable to leave.

And then the dark man saw her.

His brows went up, the cruel mouth went down; the rest was a dim blurred nightmare of horror. She had fled from them blindly, spurred by panic — by the look of their faces; and always the dark man thumped behind her and her father's shrill cursing turned her blood to water. She found a door before her and she jerked it open and rushed out into the cool night air.

Chapter 14

Tune, reaching for Tampa's hat where it lay half concealed under Lou's desk, heard the girl's shearing cry, heard the window back of him burst into shards and then all other sounds were hammered insensible by the nervesledging crash of pistol fire. Splinters stood up on the desk before him. Holes appeared in its side like magic. An old coat of Lou's fell off the wall. Another shot cuffed at the brim of Tune's hat; then his own gun kicked up an angling fire and the lamp flared once in its bracket and died.

Tune, with his belly pressed flat to the floor, felt the whole back side of the building shake. Whoever it was they were out to get him. With his knees, belly, toes, with the points of his shoulders, squeezed hard against that gritty floor, Tune inched around till he faced the window. He knew when he faced it by the deeper dark round it, by the cool night air flowing over him from it. Flare of the guns played like Northern lights over it and then Safford's high angry voice smashed through it, ordering his bravos to rush the place, to storm in and take it through their sheer weight of numbers.

Tune listened with lips thinly peeled from his teeth. He crouched and held still as their boots crossed the hardpan and were chopped up and lost in the round-about echoes. But he saw no shapes in the wind harried shadows and knew by that what was in Lou's mind. Lou's strategy was plain; he meant for those men to come in through the back and drive Tune through that shot-out window.

It was a first class plan and might work if Tune waited.

But Tune had no intention of waiting. He went scrabbling backward like a crab on his belly till he felt his boots come against the rear wall. Then he got his shoulders flat against the timbers.

Safford's mob struck the door with a rebel yell. With a squealing groan it came off its hinges and was banged underfoot by the shadow-blurred shapes bounding in across it. Tune left the wall as they crowded past, hunting him — left the wall carefully and insinuated himself brazenly into their ranks and, with them, probed the curdled gloom.

Red fire gushed suddenly out of his

pistol as he drove his flame at Lou's fallen coat that was just a black smudge in the room's far corner. And all Lou's gun slammers triggered, too. Someone yelled through that murk and gunfire rocked the shack with its pounding and the acrid smoke was for all the world like a stinging canopy flung over hell.

Tune had thought being one of them would afford the best cover, and it had. Moving with them, firing with them — in every way appearing to be one of them, had served to mask his presence from them; but now he was trapped by the pressure of them round him. He had joined their ranks but he could not safely leave them — nor could he safely continue to be one of their number. Unless —

Some man outside yelled long and full and Tune went suddenly stiff in his tracks and gasped and let his knees fold under him and felt his shape fall through those crowding legs to the floor. The press milled around him and then was gone past, each man with his gun snout riveted on the dark still smudge of Lou's coat in the corner.

Tune shoved to his knees, got one leg under him and came erect. He slipped out the door like the ghost of a shadow, and he humped his pounding boots toward the brush, toward the yonder greasewood where he'd cached his horse. A shout burst out of the street, and Lou Safford's voice slammed a halt order at him, and muzzle lights bloomed, and slugs cracked through the branches round him as Tune, bent double, dived into the thicket.

The uproar of Lou's tricked men at the office came racketing through the gusty gloom, and Lou's voice yelling they had lost Tune, cursing them; and the guns, beating up a renewed thunder, as Tune snatched reins and slogged into the saddle.

But, just as he would have gone lunging out of there, just as he lifted spurred heel to slash downward, dim through the night he heard the girl's cry — the same frantic cry he had heard in the office, Panchita's voice, lifting vibrant with fright.

Tune stayed the descent of that lifted heel. He hung that way, balanced, with a hand to the horn, with his ears strained into that raucous dark trying to make out the source of the girl's scared cry.

Through the uproar he heard it again, dim through the gun sound, through the rack of men's cursing. Dimmer now and gone toward panic.

She was out on the desert. He was sure

of that. Out on the desert and running, he thought, running deeper into the drifted sand. He dug in his spurs without mercy. The Clover Cross dun went off like an arrow, with Tune crouched low he tore through the chaparral. A treble tongued shout went instantly up. Guns belted the night, streaked the gloom with cross fire. The wind from those slugs screamed high and shrill but their aim was wild and Tune sped on. With the reins in his teeth he fumbled fresh loads to his heated pistol. And then he saw the girl's shape there ahead, a vague blur, to the left of him.

His knees signaled the horse. They went rocketing toward her, and muzzle flame licked a white line past her shape. Something jerked at his vest and Tune's bleak face went indescribably wicked as he saw the dark blur come apart, gyrate wildly, and abruptly resolve into two struggling figures locked writhing below the dull shine of a pistol.

One of those twisting shapes was the girl — he could hear the fierce pant of her labored breathing.

Tune hit the ground on skidding boot-heels. The man saw him coming and tried to jerk free — succeeded, sent the girl sprawling and lifted his sixgun. Tune, reaching for his own, found it gone.

He hurled himself slanchways. Lightning winked from the crouched man's middle. The fan of that shot was a too close thing, and Tune knew the fellow would never quit firing till his gun was shot dry. And he was right.

Fire gushed red from the fellow's gun snout. But Tune was rolling too fast to target in that murky light the man had to shoot by. Before the man could slap hammer again Tune was into him, jerking him, slamming him backward in a jolting fall.

Tune held no exaggerated views of his own ability. He knew himself to be plenty tough, but he knew there were others who were probably better and this man facing him might well be one of them.

He wished he could see who the fellow was, by some trait or gesture guess whom he dealt with; but you could not tell in this cloying murk. He had a shape to deal with and, beyond that, all he could get was a hazy impression — thick muscular legs, burly shoulders, a chin-strapped hat with a floppy brim. He saw the man roll and come to an elbow, saw him shove to his knees and come off the ground. There was no glint in the man's hand now and a pleased kind of growl welled out of Tune's throat. His lips fanned out in a savage grin as they came together in a meaty impact.

The fellow took Tune's slogging fist with a grunt and shook it off and came back swinging. A left-handed jolt raked along Tune's ear and, by the feel, took the ear along with it. Then a lifted knee skidded off his thigh and Tune knew then he was in for something. He fell back giving ground with the world redly reeling, and a roll of his head barely got him clear of the too-anxious fist that went whizzing past it.

Tune lurched in. He put his knuckles hard against the man's chin — felt chin and head snap backward fiercely; but the man got that bony knee up again and excruciating pain rushed all through Tune's body, and he doubled over; and the man came boring in like a pile driver.

Those sledge-like fists reached out like pistons and all Tune's will and footwork could not keep him entirely clear. Every blow the man struck rocked Tune to his bootheels, and he caught the dull shine of the man's grinning teeth through a kind of red fog that got darker and darker.

He stumbled backward but there was no respite. Those bone-bruising fists came rocking after him in a rain of blows that was beating him senseless. Through the roaring howl that was in his head Tune knew the end could not be far off. Queer that it should come like this, that it should be a man's fists and not lead that got him . . .

It was almost over. Tune was flat on the ground, spread-eagled there, numb and past caring — or so he thought. It was the bark of the gun that brought him out of it; a gun's explosion not two feet from his head. He sensed that the girl was crouched there by him, that hers was the hand that had fired that pistol.

He heard the man's startled curse with sharpening senses; saw the blur of a shape go slamming past — heard the girl scream as the man's fist struck her.

That jerked Tune off his back like a rope — jerked him onto his shaking knees; and cold willpower alone got him onto his feet, and the man's broad back was just before him.

Instinct, or that sixth sense that is born of danger, turned the head on those burly shoulders. The man's eyes saw Tune coming. He stood in his tracks in a kind of crouch with his fencepost legs spread wide apart. And when Tune got within reach the man hit him, two brain rocking overhand jolts of lightning that exploded against Tune like sticks of dynamite, that knocked Tune off his feet like a mallet.

But the fight spark, that killing urge buried deep within him, still shed its glow in Tune's fogged brain. It dragged him up off his aching back and pulled him over onto hands and knees; and five groping fingers scoring the dust found the butt of a pistol and balefully closed on it, and balefully came up with it as the girl screamed again. Tune lurched upright, stood there swaying, trying to focus his sight through the black fog around him.

She was out there somewhere. The man was still after her, after her with a haste that had no more time for Tune. Or maybe the fellow figured Tune was done for. He had gone anyway without making sure, and that in itself spelt a need for hurry. Every move the man made seemed geared to haste. What was the pressure? What fear spurred him so? Fear of Safford's men yonder? Did he think they were after *him?* Did he think Tune one of those cursing others?

They were getting nearer. Each widening circle was bringing them closer. Was it fear of the law that rushed the man so? And why was he after Panchita, anyway?

Tune scrubbed his eyes with the back of a hand. Every fist-thumped bone in his body ached; every nerve screamed protest of further movement. But the girl was running — running blindly with panic. He could hear her now, the racking sob of her breathing, the sand muffled beat of her headlong flight.

Tune shook his head impatiently to clear it. If only he could get his damned mind to functioning!

He knew they were somewhere off to the left. Off there in the murk not far away. He was starting for there when a rush of ponies coming out from town hit a high lope of sound and he knew it was Safford's gun fighters coming, pulled this way by the recent firing.

Closer he heard the thud of a body plummeting into the warm loose sand — heard the girl's stifled cry, an exultant grunt from the man; and by this Tune guessed the man had found and caught her.

He flung himself into a shambling run.

Chapter 15

Through the crisp still dark of the moonless night came a low muted mutter of wagon wheels. The metallic click of chains came, too, and the slowed clup-clup of the tiring horses.

Gilman levered a cartridge forward. Birch Alder pulled up his neckerchief. The Ajo stage was nearing the bend, heavily climbing the grade on that long second loop of the S-curve. The creaking of harness mingled now with the chain sound as the labored breathing of the straining wheelers drew the lumbering vehicle ever nearer and nearer. Old Pap Bennett's gnarled voice could be heard lifted occasionally above his chawing to snarl some sulphurous curse at his horses; and the bite of the iron-rimmed wheels in the roadway.

The Ajo stage was arriving at last.

They could see it now through the interstices of the dark massed foliage flanking the road, could see it coming slowly behind the plodding horses. They could make out the shotgun guard beside Pap, with his chin slid down on his chest, head bobbing.

"It's about time," the girl said, and both men looked at her.

There was something about Birch Alder's shape that suggested reluctance, a kind of unease. "Are you sure you want to go on with this?"

"Why shouldn't I want to?" The girl's voice was sharp.

Birch hesitated. "Well . . . you bein' a woman, an' all —"

"What's that got to do with it?"

"Well . . . but if it ever got out —"

"Who's going to let it out? *You're* not thinking of talking, are you? Look here," she said. "Put yourself in my place. Should I sit there at home with my hands primly folded and let Jess Crowly run me off this range?"

"You don't know it's Jess Crowly —"

"All right. So I'm guessing. It's the Seven Keys, anyway —"

"You don't even know that."

"Maybe *you* don't know it but *I'm* losing cattle! *I'm* losing horses! Men have quit me and left the country; some of my men have simply vanished! At work in the morning and gone by noon! I'm getting mine back any way that I can!"

"There's other ways," Birch Alder said earnestly. "Stickin' up stages ain't no chore for a girl — you wanta be another *Belle Starr?*"

"If you're afraid —"

"Hell! I ain't afraid of anything!"

"For a man that ain't scared you do a heap of talking."

"If I act like I'm scared," Birch growled, "it's *you* I'm scared for. What you going to do if you git shot? How you figurin' to explain off a gun wound?"

"I'm not going to have to. C'mon! Let's get at it!"

Birch didn't like it a little bit. He liked neither the business nor her attitude toward it. She was too damned cool — too hard! Like granite!

He didn't know as he *liked* girls that way. There were a lot of things Birch could countenance, but he had strong notions on the fitting and proper in regard to a woman, and he hated to see these notions tromped on. Some way her talk got under his skin. He was all mixed up in his mind and — Hell! he didn't know what he thought hardly. But if anyone had told him so recent as yesterday he'd be robbing a stage at the whim of a woman he'd have told that fool to get his head looked at!

Birch didn't see anything funny about it. It made him feel like riding plumb out of the country — and he'd have done it, too, only then it might look like she had had something, hinting he was scared. And it wasn't that he was yellow — or was it? Was it the thought of robbing this stinking stage that was bringing this clammy sweat out on him?

The time taken up by Birch in this thinking was infinitesimal — no longer, in fact, than it took him to turn and climb into his saddle. He was a man of strong hunches and the hunches were hounding him, urging him fiercely to ride and get out of this. But he quietly put his horse through the brush and eased it down to the road with Gilman's.

He wondered what Gilman was thinking.

With the sweat feeling cold underneath his collar he drew his Winchester and stepped with Gilman to the center of the road.

"Halt!" Birch shouted; and Gilman's rifle jumped to his shoulder and flame gouted whitely out of its muzzle, the reports fanning into the squeal of brake blocks.

The Ajo stage careened to a stop. Dust billowed up in a dun colored gale and the guard was cursingly hunting his shotgun

155

when Gilman's rifle streaked flame again. The guard straightened up like a rope had jerked him. The buckling hinges of his knees let go and dropped him forward between the squatting wheelers who screamed their fright and went lashing into a terrified tangle.

Pap Bennett said "Hell!" and grabbed up the shotgun, and Alder's swung rifle knocked him off the box. That was when both doors of the stage banged open and spewed out Seven Keys hands like hornets, and each of those erupting men was triggering. Birch fell wordless out of the saddle and Gilman's scream was lost in the uproar.

Behind the dark massed screen of the chaparral, Larinda McClain clapped spurs to her horse and fled, badly shaken, into the night.

Chapter 16

Tune paused once to stare through the murk while he hefted the weight of the gun in his hand. He had no remembrance of how it had got there, of how he had found it deep in the dust; and without even thinking what his fingers were doing he emptied its cylinder and filled the bored holes with cartridges fumbled fresh from his belt. And all this while he was listening, gauging, measuring the speed of those oncoming ponies against this thing which he knew he must do. Blood and death crowled through this night and a little more blood would not make much difference to a man already doomed to be hanged.

Dust was a lifted smell on the wind and, cocking his throbbing head that way, he caught the slap of flesh on flesh, the panting grunt of breaths hard caught, the beat and thud of boots swift tramping; and a senseless surge of anger plunged him forward again in that shambling run.

He could not guess, and told himself bitterly he did not care, why this blue-eyed gitana should be always in trouble. She was none of his business and he hotly resented the attraction she had for him. His mind, he thought, was a sight too keen on weaving a web of mystery around her, on building her up into something of glamor just because she was young and on her own in this country. On her own? He didn't even know that for sure. After all, she had that damn sheepherding uncle!

By grab, he'd trouble enough to look out for without going around with his mind full of gypsies. Trouble with him, he'd been too long alone; his animal hungers were painting him pictures. To a man two years on the dodge like he'd been, *any* girl would probably look like a million! He was a fool to waste thought on her. Man on the dodge had no right to a woman — no right to even be *thinking* about one; and he was already involved in the worries of one woman. But the girl with the golden hair was paying him. That made it a job and took it out of the realms of this other thing.

Thought of a woman was an obvious weakness and, if it got known, could be used against him. It could trap a man and spill his blood and get him put into a hole in the ground. Weakness was a luxury no man on the dodge could afford.

The girl was in trouble so he had to help her. She had helped him; he had to pay that back. But that was all there was to it — it had *better* be all there was to it! Her being Panchita had nothing to do with it.

He found it important that he get this matter straightened out in his mind. And, while he was still trying to do so, he saw them up in the gloom ahead — two dark lurching twisting shapes, panting, grunting, wildly swaying as they fought with the fury of desperation. The girl, lithe and wiry, was hard as an eel to grab and hang onto, and she fought with the strength of panic. But panic was not enough, nor was courage. Slowly the man's brute weight was telling. He had hold of her now. He was forcing her backward, bending her savagely, deliberately striving to snap her spine. That purpose shouted from every braced line of him, from the arched bulging muscles, from the grunt of his breathing.

"Let her go," Tune said.

Emotion, passion — the battered shape of his lips, made Tune wonder for a moment if the voice were his own. A rough wind was shouldering out of the south and the hoof-slapped sound of those onrushing ponies came stronger and stronger across the land. But the man heard Tune's words, understood their meaning. He let the girl drop. He snapped broad shoulders square around and crouched in his tracks with a hung-up breathing. He was a black silhouette against the sand and, because for the past two peril-packed years he had stayed alive by the skill of his ability to translate men's postures, Tune knew the fellow was going to leap.

He was — he did!

Even as the man's booted feet left the ground Tune brought up his pistol and squeezed the trigger. There was no mercy in him. The man deserved none and Tune meant to kill him. He pulled the trigger with a remorseless savagery. When your life is at stake you do not worry overmuch about anything but saving it.

But pulling the trigger did not save Tune's then. The pin of the hammer never touched the cartridge. The gun's mechanism jammed. The gun was filled with grit.

Tune swore. It was too late now to get out of the way. He had barely time to drop to his knees. The man's knees came hard against Tune's shoulders and half the breath was spilled out of Tune. But his wits were at work and he rolled — rolled for dear life to get clear of those fingers, those fingers that could ball into rock hard fists; and he came up onto his feet, eyes glinting, and swung with the pistol.

He felt the barrel carome against the man's beefy shoulder. He heard the grunt jounced out of the man's burly throat. But the man did not quit. He kept boring in, harshly growling, bear like, every blow he landed shaking Tune to his bootheels. The man's staying powers were terrific — maddening. It was like fighting a nightmare. Nothing you tried could prevail against it. Those killing, hammering fists kept coming.

Then a knife gleamed suddenly in the man's upraised hand. Tune felt it's edge down the length of his arm, like the bite of hot iron from wrist to elbow. He staggered sideways. The man bored in. Again that lifted blade was coming. But a lucky blow of Tune's pistol loosed it — sent it spinning off into the brush. And a change came suddenly into this fight.

Tune sensed it in the lessened ferocity of the man's bull rushes. He was no longer giving everything he had; it was as though he were fighting with only half his interest. You got the impression the man was listening, trying to gauge this thing by the sounds of impact — but that was crazy.

Then Tune got it. The man *was* listening! He was trying to gauge what time he had before those horsebackers should come up with them. You could hear them out there beating the bushes.

It was unthinking impulse that lifted Tune's voice. "Here he is!" he yelled. "Right over here, boys!" And off in the darkness, hoof sounds lashed the dust like thunder. Safford's pack came tearing headlong.

Tune grabbed for the man, bitterly cursing his folly. He wanted to be caught no more than this other man! His fingers slipped from the bulging shoulders — caught in his shirtfront; but the fellow tore loose and bounded away. He was lost in the dark, in the thunder of horse sound.

Tune knew by its feel what lay gripped in his fingers. Knowledge burned the palm of his hand. The thing he held was another of those buttons he had picked off the floor of Grankelmeir's stable! And he'd let the guy go!

Through the pain of his arm, through the arches of his body, Tune burned with that knowledge. That had been the man — he was sure of it; the knife-wielding killer of Teal and Wilkes. It explained why the fellow was after this girl. It explained a whole lot of things. Panchita had been in the stable when Teal had been stabbed. He had known it, or guessed it, and that was why he'd been after her!

Tune had no time to think further then.

The girl's hand came from the darkness and touched him. "Quick! *Andale* — hurry!"

He followed her into the whirling shadows.

He stumbled after her, impotently cursing.

Chapter 17

With the sprinting speed of a Quarter Horse, doom swept the Oro Blanco country. It fell like a darkness over the land, and no man knew where next it would strike unless perchance, that man was Jess Crowly. The hour was come, and not even to further mature his plans, or to consolidate his forces, dared Jess delay the avalanche longer. The iron was hot and he must strike. Clover Cross had dug up the hatchet and further delay might cost dark Jess not only his goal but his very life; for Tune had again slipped through his hands and there was no guessing what the man might try now.

But Tune had served Crowly well after all. Regardless of job or capacity, the man was obviously associated with Clover Cross. Jess could daub them from hell to breakfast with all the infamy of this man's reputation. But he need no longer depend on that. At last Clover Cross had come out from cover and had committed last night an act of lawless violence beyond excuse or repudiation. They were a pack of thieves and murderers and no court in the land but would back him up in it. They had stuck up the Ajo stage with rifles, faces masked with neckerchiefs, and four men lay dead as the immediate result. They had killed the shotgun guard. They had shot Pap Bennett down like a dog, and would have got clean away with the Seven Keys payroll but for the canny foresight of long-headed Jess who had put several men on the coach as passengers. These had surprised the robbers, had shot down two of them, Birch Alder and a man named Gilman, both well known to be Clover Cross hands. There had been some more of them back in the brush, but they had fled.

Crowly had good right to feel pleased. That stage job last night had turned the trick for him. Clover Cross had come out from cover and now no man could rightly blame Jess no matter what devilment came of this. The rivers could run blood red. Human bones could lie picked and bleached and no man could call Jess Crowly accountable. He might have to shoot a few people, he might have to run a few out of the country, but only in defense of his rights and interests, and whatever he did it would have the law's sanction. Jess Crowly would be acting in self-defense.

Things had really moved last night. Folks had gone plumb haywire, it looked like. Open warfare had broken out. Arson and anarchy had stalked through the land. Ten or twelve men had been dropped with their boots on, gunned by the greed of that red-jawed wolfpack that was holed up at Clover Cross and led by that renegade Texican, Tune. Whether he took his orders from himself or the girl made little difference; if the McClain girl didn't approve his acts his name would not be on her payroll.

Down valley, a pair of masked riders had ridden into a small farmer's holdings and burned him out. Had he offered resistance they would probably have killed him — they were that breed of men. Half a dozen miles east another weedbender, New Ground McCune, had been shot on his doorstep and riddled with bullets, with a rockweighted note left upon his body ordering all dirt farmers to pull their freight under threat of being fed the same medicine. Four men, riding horses marked with the Clover Cross brand, had slaughtered a herd of cows belonging to the Bar O, and had hamstrung four of the outfit's best saddlers; and the rancher's twelve-year-old daughter, left alone in the house, had been scared half senseless.

In mid-morning, a man on a lathered bronc came tearing into town hunting Crowly. After speaking with him Crowly had smiled his feline little smile. He had beckoned a couple of his handiest gun slingers and sent them off with the man on fresh horses. Then Jess went home and changed his clothes.

Men were riding all over the range that day. Rumor was rife. Crowly heard each story of pillage and arson with a face that hourly grew more indignant. At times he would pound his fist on the table and the cords in his neck would swell like ropes as he listened to the outrageous stories brought him.

Such things were not to be countenanced. Such deeds cried aloud for punishment. Clover Cross should pay to the last steer packing their brand, he swore. If the law couldn't do anything the Seven Keys would!

But first the law must be given its chance. There was a brand new sheriff in the saddle today. Lou Safford, the former Blanco marshal, had just been appointed and expected the co-operation of every honest man in the country. And he would get it, too! There would be a mass meeting held this afternoon. Until then . . .

Chapter 18

When Tune first went stumbling after the girl it seemed a thin hope to try and outrun Lou Safford's horsemen. But the girl soon proved she wasn't trying to outrun them. She was trying to elude them, to evade, get away from them — to lose them in the brush and cat-claw that here abounded so thickly and tangled the place more resembled a jungle than desert. She seemed to know what she was doing, too, and her way of doing it bred new hope in him, and he followed her with increasing confidence as, through the wind harried shadows, she led him off along an old rabbit run that angled through the slapping branches and took them deeper into the desert. He was amazed at her seeming knowledge of the country; he could not reconcile it with the fact of her so-recent arrival.

"It was Tio Felix who showed me this trail. I always take it on my trips to town. It is a short cut from our camp near Clover Cross. Tio Felix was born in this country. He was brought up on a part of

168

the Clover Cross range."

The old man's father, it seemed, had once had a ranch here, but had been driven out by Tim McClain when the Clover Cross still was building. "That is why," the girl said, "he was glad to come back here with sheep to eat the Clover Cross grass. They have played on his hatred of the McClains — on his bitterness. He has taken care of me ever since — But, quick! We must hurry — no time for talk now. We must make him see how these men are using him — You have that button?"

Tune grunted; kept casting quick looks at their backtail. "We'll never make your camp without horses —"

"But we will *have* horses!"

"What kind of Aladdin's Lamp are you packin'?"

Panchita laughed softly. "That Aladdin! He was smart — Tio Felix is, too; you will see. Just a mile or so now — just a little way more. We will both have horses — good ones! There is a gulch up ahead that has a little cave in it and that is where we keep the horses — these extra ones — 'just in case,' as Tio Felix says. Sometimes the saints are too busy to hear one."

Already, Tune noticed, the trail was tipping downward. Its descent, at first, was barely perceptible. Then it dropped more rapidly until, abruptly, Tune found himself in a narrow gorge whose walls, at the top, were almost joined together. It was very dark down here. It made the stars seem nearer, brighter. The girl moved along with a sure-footed grace, pausing to warn Tune every little while of some snaky turn or fallen boulder. And every now and again they could hear the rumor of traveling horses.

But Tune, for the time, had forgotten Lou Safford. A paralysis gripped his mind, born of exhaustion — of the battering he'd taken; and all his aching bones and muscles, every dog-tired nerve and sinew, was lifting up its agonized howl at each new-added foot of their progress. How blessed it would be just to drop in his tracks, just to welcome oblivion for ever and always and never have to get up again.

In the ghostly unreal light of this gulch he could barely make out the girl's shape before him, but something about the free swing of those shoulders was balm to Tune, like a breath of cool air through the down-smashing slant of a noonday sun. It was someway remindful of other and happier days in the past before San Saba, and all that town stood for, had shoved him onto the Boothill Trail.

Shoved him onto it? No, it hadn't done that; a man made his own kind of hell in this world. Only Tune himself could be held accountable for where Tune's boots had taken him. No use to put the blame elsewhere. Society might set up fancy rules, custom might dictate modes of conduct, but a man lived by his own conceptions and by his own acts, or failure to act, shaped and surcharged the world he lived in. If that world be not to his liking let him look to his own lone past to find where his boot left the hardpacked trail.

Tune saw that now. Too many times since that fatal night had he relived the past to mistake where the faults of the present had sprung from. He had been a fool to sign over that ranch — he had been a fool to think he needed that drink. If he'd never stepped into the Grubstake Saloon he would not be tramping this black gulch now; so it all came back to a man's own doing. Man made his own bed and, if he was a man, he climbed into it.

Which was not to say Tune felt less bitter toward the man who had taken advantage of his trust. Tune was growing, all right, but he had not grown that much.

He hated Stokes with a bitter intensity and if ever Stokes' trail cross his again it was going to be just too bad for somebody!

The girl's voice roused him.

Her hand was on Tune's arm and, even through the lethargy of pain and exhaustion that draped his mind as with tatters of fog, he could feel her tremble — could hear the sharp gasp of her indrawn breath as, instinctively, she shrank away from him. It came to him then with a sense of bewildered surprise that he was no longer walking — was no longer on his feet. He was on the ground, kind of crumpled there like, with his face uncomfortably against the trail's gravel. He squirmed around, got his head off the ground; with every ounce of will he could muster he got his good right arm beneath him and worked himself up to a sitting posture. Cold sweat stood out all over him.

"You're hurt, Dakota — your arm's all blood!"

He could see the gray blur of her face bent over him.

"I guess I'm not so tough as I figured. If —"

"Wait! You cannot go on losing blood like that."

But Tune, with a growl, was grinding his boots hard against the gravel. He felt weak as a chicken but he kept on straining and finally his labor got one leg under him and, with the girl's help, he lurched erect. He stood there, swaying weakly. It was like the shakes had got into his knees and only the girl's steadying grip kept him up.

But she couldn't seem to get her mind off that blood. "Your wound, prala . . ." She said urgently: "We must tie it up!" and he felt her grip go briefly away from him, heard the rip of cloth, felt her hands come back to him; and presently she was saying, "It is not far now. Listen! You hear the horses, prala?"

Tune grunted, bearing harder and harder against her. He made a strenuous effort to get hold of himself; made a try to go on without her help but his breath came shorter and shorter and the sweat rolled into his eyes like rain and he reeled to a floundering, all-in stop.

Once more the girl's hands were on him, holding him. She got his good arm over her shoulder. "Let your weight come on me, prala. I will be your rod and your staff — it will comfort you."

A bitter laugh growled up out of him and he said between the harsh grunts of his breathing, "You've already got all the weight that's in me." He shook his head, trying to get some sense into it. "It's no good, Panchita. You go on — you go on without —"

"But it's just a little way — just around the next bend. Look! You can almost *see* it. In the right-hand wall. A tiny opening just back of the brush. There is food and blankets — Can't you make it, prala? Can't you go that far?"

She looked at him, worriedly biting her lips. For the last half mile he had leaned on her heavily, struggling on in a kind of half stupor that told her better than any words how near he was to the end of his strength. He was out on his feet, and if he fell again . . .

She wouldn't let herself think of it. "Would you rather wait while I fetch the horses?"

"No — No, I'll make it, I guess. Hang hold of me — Now then!"

They lurched on again and he wondered at her pluck, at the unexpected strength she had found for them. And then his mind quit all attempts at coherence and he was conscious of only an interminable lifting and lowering of legs that no longer had any feeling, of dragging feet that were like mud-gripped anchors.

A shallow creek purled underfoot now, swirling and gurgling around obstructions, and the cold wet feel of it partially roused him. He tried to be of some help to himself as the girl carefully guided him over and around the slipperiest stones.

They stumbled out of the water at last and onto a shelving beach, and heard the near-by nicker of horses. There was a smell of damp and growing things and the night seemed not so dark as it had been.

"We're almost there," Panchita said. "Just a few more steps — just behind that brush over there to the right"; and he went staggering after her through the wet branches and through the dark slit in the canyon wall.

The horses made whinnying sounds of welcome. The girl struck a match and found a candle stump in a bottle, and lit it. He saw the horses then, a pair of them. Chesty sorrels. They were penned in a corner roped off for them, and there was baled hay spilled on the ground about them; and these familiar smells of hay and horses gave to the place a homey feeling that was infinitely soothing.

There was a welter of blankets dumped in a corner and Panchita helped him over there, and his knees let go and dropped him onto them. He smiled tiredly, his cheeks faintly edged with color, that he was so little able to control his actions. And Panchita said, "Rest. God will look out for you. I will find Tio Felix and bring —"

That was all Tune heard. Exhaustion had its way with him. Sleep drugged his eyes and he heard no more. He did not hear the girl saddle or go; he did not know how she first stood and looked at him, or how changed and reserveless her eyes then became before she turned away, oddly wistful, and left him.

It was late afternoon when Tune opened his eyes. His body felt like it had been through a rock crusher and pain knifed through him when he moved his cut arm, but his head — thank God! — was clear at last.

He placed the time by the look of the sunlight spilling in through the slit in the wall. It filled the cavern with a mellow glow that was like the intensified flare of a lantern. He guessed it was probably the restive stomping of the gelding which had roused him.

But it wasn't.

His first intimation of danger came when

he, very carefully, started to get up. A booted weight ground the shale of the floor. A man's voice said, "Take it easy, bucko. You ain't goin' no place."

The jerked turn of Tune's shoulders was hard enough and quick enough to send hot pain rushing through his arm. And what he saw pulled his breath up short.

There were two men watching him, flanking the speaker. The man who had spoken Tune knew by sight. A wire-thin shape in a pinto vest with two forty-fours strapped around his middle — a very hard customer. Loma Jack Marana was the name he went by. He'd been a one-time boss of the border dope runners, though right now he wore a deputy's badge and was palpably enjoying the airs that went with it.

Light yellowed his cheek bones and threw back its brightness from cat-lidded eyes that were tawny and watchful and aglint with amusement. He said, "I'll take that gun you got stuck in yore pants, Tune."

Tune shrugged, saying nothing. He made no move to produce it.

Loma Jack rolled a smoke with his cat-sly eyes going over Tune blandly. He said, "Skeet, go get it," and one of the gun toughs siding him slid forward and got it and went sneeringly back with it.

Tune, still motionless, appeared outwardly calm and wholly indifferent.

Loma Jack raked Tune with his hard yellow eyes. "Takes a heap of imaginin'," he said, "to fit some guys to their reps around here." Then he said in his quick, sharp, arrogant way: "Where's the girl?"

"What girl?"

"Come on — come on," the gun boss growled. "Do I got to fetch you a look at her picture?" He sifted a handful of grit and said, "When I shove you a question, by God you answer! Get off them blankets!"

Tune got up, but he managed it badly. He did not quite smother the groan that came out of him.

"You're liable to have somethin' to groan about if you don't git that jaw to workin'. Where-at's that girl?"

Tune shook his head. He said reasonably, "If you mean the McClain girl . . . ?"

Loma Jack just looked at him. "Okey," he said. "By God, if you want it the hard way, bucko — I guess you better be showin' him that charm, Skeet."

The fat-faced Skeet moved up to Tune again.

"Look here," he said, thrusting out his

left hand; and when Tune looked, Skeet hit him. Between the eyes and it wasn't a love pat.

When Tune got his eyes pried open again he was flat on his back on the lumpy floor staring up at a roof that was swinging in circles. His face was wet, and his hair and shirt, and he knew how come when he saw Skeet chuck a bucket in the corner.

The gun boss said, "You better be givin' a little thought to this, bucko."

The man's hardcases grinned, and Tune painfully got himself off the floor and it wasn't just acting that made him groan this time.

Loma Jack smiled pleasantly. "Where's the girl, Mister Tune?"

Tune dragged his good hand across his face and wished Loma Jack's wiry shape would quit jumping. Then the three shapes presently settled into focus, but the place where Skeet had hit him felt raw and bloated. He put careful fingers up to it gingerly and almost passed out from the blinding pain of it. When the gun boss' face got still again Tune looked at the blood on his fingers and winced.

Loma Jack said: "You goin' to talk, or ain't you?"

"I don't know where she is," Tune said.

"You come here with her —"

"But I was out when she left."

"I expect you could guess where she went if you tried, mebbe."

Tune said nothing.

Anger darkened Loma Jack's lean cheeks. He looked at the fat-faced Skeet and nodded.

Skeet stepped over. A grin tugged his lips.

Tune said, "If you smack me again you better make it damn final."

"Now look," Loma Jack said earnest like. "I could kill you as easy as guttin' a slut. But what would be the good in it? I got nothin' ag'in' you, personal. So here's what I'll do. I'll make you a trade. You give me your word to get out of the country — and tell me where that damn girl has gone — an' you can climb on that geldin' an' get the hell out of here."

His cat-yellow eyes went over Tune carefully. "Well? What you say? Is it a deal?"

"I don't make deals with polecats."

Color crept blackly through the gun boss' cheeks. Flame flecks showed in the narrowed eyes and his jaw came forward heavily, angrily. Standing that way he made a dark crouching wedge against the refracted sun glow; there was in the fixity of his posture a quality that was more ominous than any spoken threat. His fists splayed out above the butts of his pistols and he looked in that moment exactly what he was, a killer who killed for the sheer lift it gave him.

He began to shake with the passion inside him.

His right hand dipped, whisked a gun from leather. He stood like that with his whole face working and the heavy six shooter waggling in his hand. "By God," he snarled, "you ain't a-goin' to have her! You got one slut an' she's enough for you! That blue eyed tidbit belongs to me and by God I'll have her! I been chasin' round after her long enough. If I don't get her then I swear t' Christ there won't *no*body get her! An' that goes fer Jess Crowly, too, by God!"

Tune heard his wild talk without remark. The man's whole shape was shaking. Sweat was a shine on that writhing face and the veins at his temples were swollen and purple. His bloated face was not an arm's length from Tune; and, outside, the sun shone bright and warm and the creek ran its joyful way, softly gurgling. Here in this glowing cliffside pocket the flies were droning their interminable song, and the chestnut gelding was restively stamping his unshod feet and hopefully waiting for the time when freedom would send him whirling out over the desert miles.

But there was no freedom possible for the man who stood in Dakota Tune's boots; and Tune knew that. There was just the bare chance of a few more hours before some gun, or the law, finally got him. Yet he found in retrospect that life was still precious, still something to be cherished and fought for; and he brought his right hand naturally up from the waist and brushed his moist cheeks with the back of it. And he observed the set placement of Loma Jack and his gun-dogs, and he felt the hot wind that kept flapping the pages of a yellowed paper; and then he sent that raised arm in an outward arc that quit like a rock against Skeet's fat face and sent the man staggering across the floor. And Tune's other arm, that pain-shot left one, came up like a mallet, unsettling the aim of Loma Jack's pistol; and Tune seized that pistol and wrenched it away from him as the man doubled up with Tune's knee in his crotch. Tune, whirling then, brought that seized gun across the third man's face in a vicious swipe that wilted him down like a tallow candle.

The gun boss caught his breath and his

balance. Curses spilled from his writhing lips and he clawed his second gun out of its leather; and the bloody-faced Skeet, half across the room, came onto a knee with a lifting pistol; and the gelding reared, squealing, in a frenzy of terror while sixguns crashed and bullets whined in ricochet and the weaving shadows of men's frantic shapes played out the pattern of foreordained fate.

Crouching, Tune dived for the sunlit portal, for that water-cut gash in the standstone wall. The gun boss' pistol bucked in his hand, that shot brushing blood from Tune's ear to his cheekbone; and Tune knew then how unlikely it was that he ever would really get out of this, but he fought on, working his trigger till the gun clicked empty, firing into that smoking maelstrom.

He was a lone, crouched shape bluely wreathed in gunsmoke whose bared teeth gleamed through bitter lips. He shot to kill and he shot without mercy. These men's only code was kill or be killed; they knew nothing else, cared for nothing better. They were border vermin — breed of the chaparral; and all Tune's thoughts in that hideous moment were for the one who waited in trust that he would save her, that yellow-haired girl back at Clover Cross.

He fired till his gun clicked empty; and he saw the fat Skeet suddenly wilt in his tracks and spill grotesquely through the swirls of powder smoke. He saw Loma Jack drop behind baled hay, horribly cursing, epileptically mouthing; and he waited no better chance. He flung himself through that brush-grown slit, tumultuously he went through it and out into the hot sun-gilded open, and found it good just to be alive.

Three ground hitched horses were not ten feet off, the mounts of Loma Jack and his crew. The animals looked up expectantly, one swinging its head down and pawing at the ground. Tune looked them over, swiftly noting their points. He picked the one that was pawing, the apron-faced bay. He would chouse off the others, drive them with him to choke off at the start any chance of pursuit. Then he shook his head, remembering the chestnut gelding, the big-boned sorrel, that was still in the cave for Loma Jack to use if he were still in shape to climb into a saddle.

So Tune started for the horses, fumbling his shell belt to find fresh loads. He could still hear Loma Jack's vicious cursing. The man was alive yet, anyway.

He had just shoved the last load into his pistol and was beside the forward-pricked ears of the bay. He was lifting a hand to reach for the horn when a group of riders burst round the bend. They saw him and yelled, and one loud voice, Lou Safford's bull bellow, sailed against the rocks and the whole bunch started triggering.

The bay jerked once and dropped dead in its tracks.

Chapter 19

When he saw that shudder writhe through the bay's frame, even before the struck animal started to fall, Tune knew this was it — the end of the trail. With Loma Jack, or one of Jack's gun throwers, due any moment to burst out of that cavern, with Safford's bleach-eyed wolfpack deputies avidly watching him over their gun sights, nobody had to tell Tune he was licked. He stood there, upright, beside the bay's body and saw the end of all he had run from, the end of each dream, of each thing he had fought for; and he realized then what a fool he had been. He should have known he was whipped from the very start. This was the end Blackwell Stokes had planned for him, the end of a fugitive, the gunsmoke payoff. The inevitable end of an owlhoot rider.

He would have surrendered then but for the chessy-cat grin on Lou Safford's face.

This was Lou's proud moment. This afternoon's work would reinstate him in the eyes of all those who had seen him humbled. Tune stood trapped, straight and plain in the open, and by his rock Lou grinned derisively. He had been a long while on this fellow's trail, all the way from faroff Atchison, but now he was come up with him; the end was in sight and it looked good to Lou. Out here in the brush Lou could make the account balance. These weren't cattlemen, these men who rode with him; they were a breed of the chaparral — gun toughs, vultures, and would care precious little what happened to Tune. They would care no more than they cared for justice, for the even break, for the rules that guided more solid citizens. Tune was nothing but cash in their pockets, and he would not be that until they had him dead.

A few looked at Safford and Safford nodded. Lead sang its song through the evening sun.

Thoughts come sometimes faster than light, and that was the way it was with Tune as he stood and watched. The bay horse fall. He had his small regrets in that moment and he thought of the girl; and then the guns started pounding the cliffs again and he dropped by the horse and raised his pistol.

Lou's men on their horses made mighty good targets until he had hammered a pair from their saddles; then panic jumped in and changed that charge through a brainless milling into headlong flight. But even as Lou's men whirled crazed horses, a gun began blasting from the brush back of Tune. Its lead hit the bay like blows from a cleaver. Lou's men took heart and came back to their purpose. Tune, counting himself already dead, whirled up on his feet and flung two shots at the cavern portal. Loma Jack went suddenly back out of sight with his mouth spread wide in a soundless yell.

Like a flash Tune ducked and rolled for cover. Lead snapped brush all around his body and, twice, slugs ripped gouts out of his chaps. Then he was back of a rock and jamming fresh loads in his smoking pistol.

Safford's men grabbed the lull to fling down off their horses. They dropped out of sight behind nearest cover, melting like dew under the lash of sun. Tune lifted his head two inches and saw nothing. He drew a deep breath into his sweat-streaked body and lifted his head a full half hand higher.

"Come out of there, Tune," Safford yelled. "Come out of there!"

Tune said dryly, "Come get me." And he peered again, cautiously, around his rock and through the ferned foliage of a low mesquite. But no men showed but the two he had dropped in that first swift exchange, and these did not show any prevailing interest.

"What's the matter with you — scared?" Safford taunted.

"You bet!" Tune said. "I'm scared you ain't going to get out of this, Lou."

"If you'd get up onto your hind legs and fight —"

"I'll get up any time you want to stand with me. I'm not worrying much about them rats you've got with you, but any time you want to make —"

"Words!" Safford scoffed. "I come out here hunting a hell-bending sheriff-killer, and all I find is a goddam windbag! You better come out of there while you're able."

Tune could hear him whispering with some of his outfit. Came the sound of a hard-galloped horse, swiftly fading; and Tune wondered uneasily where and for what Lou had sent that man dashing. His arm ached intolerably. He cuffed the sweat from his eyes with torn knuckles.

This was it, all right. This was going to be it unless he found some way of getting out of here pronto. There was a cold in his bones that the sun didn't get to, and he found himself kind of wondering about that. He had never felt premonition so keenly.

Then, across this thinking, stole the piquant features of the blue eyed gitana; and he wondered if she had found Tio Felix and whether she had made the sheep boss see how these crooked sons were using him, were using his hatred of Clover Cross to help them smash that grand old ranch. Very probably, Tune thought, he would never know. Just another unsolved mystery. Just one more of those things for the mind to pick at, like that one fleeting glimpse of stark emotion he had caught in the eyes of the yellow-haired Larinda. So plain he could remember her! So vividly he could yet see that look that had been in her eyes as she had stared down upon the lifeless clay of her brother stretched stark and still on the spur-scarred planks of the Crockett House porch.

Thought of the girl brought fresh sweat to Tune's cheeks. No telling what deviltry Crowly was hatching. Having set his new sheriff to tracking down Tune, he was not of the kind to be lolling idle. Even now he might be raiding Clover Cross, might be gutting the place, bent on ruining it utterly as a warning for other stubborn ranchers.

But, romantic and fine as the old spread was, it was no feeling for the ranch that shaped Tune's look. It was plight of the girl, of yellow-haired Larinda so slim and straight in the face of odds; it was of the undreamed lengths to which Crowly might go . . . of the things he might do . . . of the shame —

"God!" Tune breathed, and it was like a prayer. It was a desperate wail flung against these winds — against these winds of adversity, against the creek's gurgling racket and the suddenly increased sound of gunfire that was sweeping from Lou's snarling wolf-pack.

They were coming for him now. They were stealthily creeping through the grasses, creeping round the boulders, creeping through the branches — maybe even through the gurgling waters of the creek; creeping, creeping, with all a spider's noiseless stealth suddenly to pounce and sink their fangs in him, to close his eyes while the sun was bright and warm overhead and the earth beneath his shape was moist and smelling of green things growing . . .

The sparkling creek ran shining past and in his veins Tune's blood turned cold and sluggishly moved like boot-churned slush;

and a crazy impulse jerked him up and muscular reaction grabbed him suddenly and flung him headlong through the brush and toward that half screened gash of the cavern he had so lately left with the hope of a freedom. It was a desperate long-odds chance for a horse that was sending him back, the last-hope chance of a man long doomed.

He scoffed at himself, for the sorrel was dead. It *had* to be — in his heart Tune knew it. What horse could have lived through such leaden hail as had ricocheted off those rocky walls with Tune and Jack's gun hawks shooting it out?

He dashed for the cavern anyway, well knowing the chance he took in this. There was no chance at all back there in the rocks on that shelving beach. Sheer amaze must have frozen Lou's men in their tracks. They let him get almost out of their sight before their guns started up again.

If that horse still lived — that sorrel gelding — and Tune could get a leg over its back . . .

Thought of that animate barrel under him, of the joy of those fast legs bearing him off, brought new life to Tune's leaden limbs. By the narrow cleft of the cavern's entrance he whirled and loosed a couple more shots, and saw one man throw his arms out wildly. Then he jumped Loma Jack's sprawled moveless shape and threw himself inside the portal, and change in light for an instant stopped him with his back hard shoved against the nearest wall. The place swung into grim focus and he glimpsed the fat Skeet on two knees and an elbow trying to stuff fresh shells in a pistol.

The man jerked up the gun and fired.

Tune saw the flame gout out of its muzzle. But the shot jarred off and rock dust dribbled down from the roof as Tune's lifted boot took the man in the throat and slammed him into his rising partner. Both men went down in a squirming heap and the squirmer, the bloody-faced man Tune had hit on the head, was too fight drunk to leave it there and madly reached for the gun Skeet had dropped.

Tune let him have it — and a bullet with it, and the man's long shape folded floorward loosely. Hard on the heels of this man's fall a volley came racketing through the portal, and somebody outside yelled like a maniac, and a second gunblast shrilled through the cleft and knocked chips off the sandstone walls.

It was then Tune's glance found the

sorrel gelding and he knew he had swapped the witch for the devil. He had bent all his hopes of escape on this horse, and there the horse lay, dead with glazed eyes on the cavern floor.

For a moment Tune stood with his look gray and bleak. The bones of his knotted fists showed whitely. He was trapped beyond hope. His own scuffed boots had brought him here, his own battered flesh and unbending will. But these could not get him out of this place. Safford's men could sit back and wait till hell froze; they had him now and they knew it this time. They could bottle him here till starvation killed him, till he died of thirst or of his own better thinking. They could lie in the cool of the chaparral's shade and let plain madness do their work for them.

For a man could *go* mad trapped like this!

But what of that girl with the golden hair whose first glimpsed look had brought him here? — whose desperate straits had hired his gun? — whose pride and pluck had sowed the seed whose growth had snared and kept him here?

What now of *her?* She could not wait!

And what of that other — that gypsy waif whose pluck had twice saved Tune's own life? — whose eyes were the blue of angel eyes . . .

With mouth awry Tune bitterly cursed.

Chapter 20

The wolves sat down in the chaparral to wait and Tune could hear their snarling voice sounds. These told him plain he had cut his stick too short this time.

The sun went down red as flame in the west and the sawtoothed peaks turned the color of blood. Tune's sunken eyes, deep pouched in misery, looked around the cave and uncaring saw the sprawled dead shapes; and he lurched against the wall and leaned there. A great weariness gripped him, a lethargy that took no account of time or need. He was a dead man — the one dead man who hadn't fallen. The one dead man doomed to go on thinking and feeling and caring, doomed to go on fighting though his hour had come.

His glance touched and left the last man dropped. It fastened on the fat-faced Skeet between whose eyes the hair was smeared in a wanton streak and clotted there like an actor's mask. The feel of those eyes was like a curse as they followed Tune round while he picked up the guns and flung them into the outside brush. The fat man almost cried when the last gun fell beyond his reach.

Tune went to him then and patched him up, what little he could, though the man's only thanks was that black look of hate that burned like peat in his unwinking gaze. Half of the lead Skeet packed would have killed other men. But this obese Skeet was like a broken-backed snake; he would strike if chance offered. In the venomous mind behind those eyes there was no other thought, no better wish.

Tune stood there too dog-tired to think and heard the wrangling snarls of Lou's men without even trying to make sense of them. Why had the man he had fought last night been so intent on killing the blue eyed gitana? He *had* tried to *kill* her; it *might* have been him who had tried before. Outside the walls of Madam Belladine's brothel. In the blue shadowed doorway of Riske Quentin's cantina.

But *why?*

What could that little gitana know that should make her death so imperative to him? Did she know *anything?* Or was the reason, rather, in something she had done to him, or in some thing she had failed to do?

Tune felt the two buttons that were in his chaps pocket. He fetched them out and stared at their round red shapes in his palm. Two hand carved buttons of dark mesquite wood. Alike as two peas.

With a grunt Tune put them back in his pocket and filled the emptied loops of his belt from the long row of shells that gleamed in Jack Marana's. He dragged off his hat and pitched it aside and put Loma Jack's soiled hat on his head. He peeled off his vest and painfully wriggled out of his shirt. He replaced these also from the dead outlaw's garb.

The dying Skeet came up on an elbow and his twisted lips drew back in a sneer. "Ain't you goin' to put on the dead man's boots?"

"Why not?" Tune grunted, and made the swap.

"*They* won't git you out of this." He leered at Tune wickedly. "You're a cooked goose, boy — cooked for a gal that wouldn't turn a hand for you! Cooked by the same kinda smile that cooked Jack — Oh, she had him throwin' his weight around, too, till Jess showed him what a damn fool he was. Jess'll tame her — but *you* won't be around to see it."

Skeet laughed through the clogging

blood in his throat, laughed till the tears rolled down his fat cheeks. But Dakota, after that first quick look, discounted it all for the work of venom, for the feverish imaginings of a twisted mind. He would not believe such hate ridden words. Maybe she *had* tried to hire Jack's guns — it was convincing proof of her desperation; but that she could see any — "Phah!" Tune grimaced. She was not the one to trade herself like a stinking Judas for a sackful of coins! She had no call to sell herself, to pass out her favors for a little help. A man's help was her due, it was a man's acknowledgment of her high character, of her sweetness and goodness, resolution and pluck.

Skeet's talk was wild. It sprang from a plain wish to hurt Tune — that was it! From the man's wicked wish to make Tune think he had thrown away his chance to help out a woman who wasn't worth helping . . .

Tune suddenly spun with eyes gone narrow and stared intently toward the last shine of sun where it gilded the thorny brush by the passage. One word from that outside welter of talk had cut through his thinking. One word.

Dynamite!

It had been Lou's voice that had used the word. Lou's voice, quick and terse with command; and now another rider was pelting off, was clattering over the creekside shale and pounding away to do Lou's bidding.

Dynamite!

That was the answer. That was how they aimed to be rid of him.

That was Lou, all right. That was Lou every time. Play it safe! Lou could polish Tune off very neatly with dynamite. Dynamite would not tie Lou to it. He should have expected smart Lou to think of that. He would call on Tune to surrender and, when Tune refused to come walking out to him, he would throw his bundle of yellow sticks and the result would be all anyone could ask for. It would be the same if Tune *did* surrender. For they would then pin Loma Jack's death on him — a deputy killed in performance of duty.

The game was Lou's any way you played it.

Tune turned with a shrug and met Skeet's eyes. "They're bringing in dynamite," he said. "Fetchin' it up from one of the abandoned mines. If you want to get out of this I'll give you a hand —"

Skeet grinned. "Not on your life! I

wouldn't miss this for a million dollars! I'll be right here with you. I want to *see* you die!"

Tune said with a snort, "You don't think I'll wait for it, do you?"

"You'll wait all right. I'm goin' to see that you do!"

"Yeah?"

"You know it! First try you make to get yourself out of here I'm goin' to shout my damn head off. Get it?"

Tune looked at the man and Skeet's twisted lips curled back off his teeth.

"I've got you pegged, boy. You don't fool me! You're tougher than fish eggs rolled in sand — but there's a soft streak in you. You been raised too good. An owlhooter's got to take care of his chances; he can't go soft like you done for that girl. You can glare your damn head off but you *can't down a man that's unarmed in cold blood.*"

He lay back with that blood-choked gurgling laugh. "You wasn't cut out for a owlhooter, boy. You ain't got the guts to take a gun now an' finish me!"

It was true, Tune realized. Skeet had called the turn.

Chapter 21

Tune stared out into the gathering dusk.

It would soon be dark. If night beat the man who had gone for that dynamite —

Night didn't.

Tune could hear the dim flutter of far-away hoofs. Safford's men, gathering stuff to build their watchfires, also heard; and they set up a cheer. They threw fresh taunts at the cavern. Swiftly the wind bore the hoofbeats nearer. Safford's men quit gathering wood and Safford's voice shoved them back to their posts again, and all was the same as it lately had been with the sound of that horse getting steadily closer.

Through the gloom Tune could feel Skeet's unwinking gaze. If he tried to get out of there Skeet would yell, thereby killing the chance. If he stayed, Safford's yellow sticks would make short work of him.

Tune stared at the man through the creeping shadows. He went over, bent down and examined Skeet's bandages.

They were sticky and the man's skin was hot as fire. Yet he wasn't delirious. He looked up at Tune with his twisted grin. "Don't worry about me. I'm goin' to enjoy this."

"Maybe so."

Skeet peered through the gloom trying to read Tune's face. Then the croaking laugh rolled again from his throat and banged thin and harsh against the rocks. "Quit churnin' your bowels. You ain't goin' no place."

"Maybe not," Tune grunted. "Roll over on your side."

Sudden fear flashed into Skeet's feverish glance. "You ain't quittin' this place . . ." He said it less certainly. He said it with something of fright in his look.

"I'm makin' my try," Tune told him. "And I'll tell you for sure it's goin' to be a good one."

"You won't like dyin' with lead in yore guts!"

"I'd as soon die of lead as of hangman's rope. Get over on your side —"

"No!" Skeet said. "No! You wouldn't dass gun me!" He licked at his stove-hot lips and cursed. "It would ha'nt you all the rest of yore days —"

"I —"

"You ain't *killed* a man, boy — you don't know what it's like! It won't be like that San Saba business. You know damn well you never killed that feller! You'll be seein' —"

Tune stopped the man's talk with an outthrust hand.

The sound of a horse clattered into the gulch. Voice sound rose, excited, exultant. Tune bent over Skeet with a sense of urgency. "Get your arm round my neck —"

"God's watchin' you, boy!"

"Quick!" Tune growled. He bent lower. "Get your arm round my neck. I'm going to lift you up."

A shudder ran through the fat man's shape. He cringed away with a blubbering snarl. He said aghast: "A human shield!" and recoiled from Tune's hand like a snake had touched him. "I won't! I won't do it — I'll yell!"

"Christ!" Tune said. "I'm tryin' to get you out of this!"

"You're not!" In the thickening murk the man's eyes looked like saucepans. He drew a ragged breath. He shook his head unbelievingly. "Mean you'd risk your neck fer a feller like me? . . . No guy could be softheaded as that — it's a ruse. *You're lyin', boy!* You want to hold me up like a shield for their bullets!"

Tune sighed. "I could whack you on the head just as well."

He dropped to his knees and got one arm half around Skeet's waist. "Let yourself relax . . . Catch hold of me now . . . I want to get you over my shoulder — that's it!" He came erect with a hard wrench of muscles. "Now then!"

With his free hand Tune got his gun from its scabbard and, crouching low under Skeet's heavy weight, staggered toward the cave's opening. On second thought he shoved the gun back in leather. Its dull gleam might show and betray their position. Safford's men would spot them quick enough anyway.

He paused by the opening to shift Skeet's weight. Safford's voice, down below, said "All right," very clearly and a concerted movement, as of men scattering out, came upslope through the night's thickening shadows.

"I'm going to try it now. Keep your face turned away from them."

Tune could feel Skeet shudder. "God's watchin' you, boy."

Tune damn sure hoped nobody else was.

He stepped through the cleft like he was treading on glass and night closed in dark and cold against him, and he was suddenly lonely and drearily wondered where all this would end. Could ever a man fully know life's answers before death tapped his shoulder and put all knowing to a final end? He tried to think what life could mean to a man like Skeet. To these gun hung men of the backtrails life could hardly be much but quick farewells, gunsmoke and sunlight and death at the end. A fading memory, perhaps, of something briefly glimpsed in a woman's eyes. He thought life must be for everyone mainly remembered glimpses of things they had never attained.

He moved into the chaparral.

Night curtained the land like a stuck-fast fog. Like a fat wet hand pushed against your face. Like the pennies laid over a dead man's eyes.

Tune could sense the shifting of Safford's men and he smiled enigmatically into the darkness. They would be watchfully spreading upslope toward him, creeping and crawling with their guns thrust before them like little black beetles with their heads to the earth. They were a definite pressure that was carefully maneuvering him. And over and above any other feeling was the threat of those yellow sticks

Lou had sent for. Any moment the world might explode in one shattering, final burst of light. Any moment Dakota Tune and one of those crawlers might come face to face across lifted guns; yet Tune dared not hurry lest his feet betray him.

His ears got tired with the strain of listening. His mind rebelled against this needed caution, yet he clung to it. He yearned to run like a deer and get out of this but he continued his tedious advance along the gulch wall, creeping over and around and, sometimes, through the bushes. A thorny branch slapped Skeet and the fat man groaned, and a challenge jumped out of the dark to their left.

A cold sweat filmed Tune's scowling cheeks and a streak of flame left the yonder murk and lead whined past his stiffened shape. But he held his fire, listening to that shot's wild echoes slamming along the canyon walls. Lou's voice came angrily up the slope and, thereafter, silence closed like a fist about them and, gradually, Tune heard again the advance of Lou's men.

He wondered why Lou did not use his dynamite. Had Lou failed to get it? Was the man's ride in vain?

That must be it, Tune thought; and

again took hope.

Yet he stayed where he was with Skeet on his back and stared toward the place the gun had flashed from. That man, angered, would be doubly alert and Tune dared not risk drawing fire again.

Then he saw a shape silently drifting toward him and the tension proved too great for Skeet and sound broke out of the fat man suddenly. Skeet's arms closed strangling tight round Tune's neck and Skeet's croaking voice cried crazily: *"Here he is! He's right amongst you. Right —"*

With a surge of strength Tune broke Skeet's hold and the man let out a shriek and slid, a loose dead weight, down the backs of Tune's legs as Lou's men loosed a rattling blast that shook the brush like a gust of wind; and shale bounced like hail off the canyon wall.

Relieved of Skeet's weight Tune ripped out his gun and fired point-blank at the shape before him. The man buckled forward and one more shot sang past Tune's face. A bullet slapped off the ground in front of him. Another cuffed a flap of his chaps.

He flung himself up the canyon trail. Three long, sprinting, rushing strides he took and was caught in the tide of charging men — black crouching shapes in the gloom crouched round them. Cursing, panting, struggling shapes with fire wreathing out of the snouts of their pistols. Dim-seen, fleeting phantom shapes that struck and swung and triggered round him. A man's shoulder hooked him hard in the chest and Tune batted that man with his gun weighted fist and saw the man's shape reel back and away from him. He stumbled headlong over another. He clawed to his feet and tried to get into the brush again but could not make it. A man welled out of the ground in front of him and Tune's brought-up knee caught him in the groin; another man got an arm round Tune's waist but Tune shook free and went plunging on.

Muzzle flame ripped and crisscrossed the darkness. Powder smell rolled with the rising wind.

And, suddenly, Tune found himself out of it. Out in the clear and running, stumbling, lurching on through the black and gusty night. Men's shouts and gun sound dimmed away.

Ahead was clean unbroken dark.

He had no idea where he was or how far he had come from that canyon shoot-out. But he was clear of the canyon. He was out on the broad sweep of desert again with its studdings of yucca and cholla and the thorn spiked branches of twisted mesquite.

He thought he had tramped for hours but the east hadn't cracked to day's coming yet. The eastern skyline was too black to see and his feet were like lead and twice as unmanageable. His legs were sticks on rusty hinges and he was never quite sure if he were lifting his feet or just making ready to set his feet down. He thought about this for a while and, when he caught himself doing so, knew how near whipped out he was.

He felt pretty sure he was going the right way. Clover Cross must be off here someplace. He was out on his feet but he wouldn't admit it. He *had* to keep going. He had to reach shelter because if daylight found him still out in this open the wasteland sun would make short work of him. Of course, the sun might not get a chance to. It wouldn't if Safford's men came across him.

His slashed arm felt like fire was in it. It was swelling, too.

Up foot, down foot — mile on reeling endless mile. Up foot, down foot; he had never guessed this desert was so big. It seemed to stretch to eternity and there were no landmarks to set a course by — not even a star shone down to guide him. He made shift to count his weary steps but there was too much sameness. It was like tramping all night on a treadmill. You made a lot of movement but you never seemed to be getting anyplace. Up foot, down foot. The same pools of shadow always ringed you round, the same marched on with you and stopped when you stopped.

Maybe, Tune thought, he wasn't moving. Maybe he just thought he was. Maybe he had stood all this time in one place.

The notion finally took such a hold of him he got down onto his hands and knees and crouched there, groggy, looking at his tracks. He stared a long while before he remembered why he was staring. But he could only find one set of tracks — a kind of wabbling, weaving, fool sort of tracks. But there was just the one set. They were his, and none of them looked to have been stepped in twice. There were no tracks ahead of him.

It took quite an effort to get up on his feet again but he finally made it and staggered on.

Up foot, down foot, up foot, down foot. Someplace a coyote lifted its voice, and other coyotes happily answered until their ululating calls made a kind of chorus, a mad symphony of sound rushing over the sand and swiftly lost.

There was a black ugly shadow up ahead a ways that Tune was sure he had passed before. It resolved, when he reached it, into a jaggedly weatherworn outcropping of sandstone. He was sure he had passed it no less than twice already; and he got down onto his knees again and commenced crawling around it in search of tracks. There were none, however — just the ones he was right then making, freakish indentations such as might have been made by Stone Age Man trying to scoop up the mental waters of a mirage.

Struggling upright Tune cursed himself for a loco fool. A fine lot of good he was doing Clover Cross! A hell of a trouble buster *he* was! Just about as much help as a twenty gauge shell in a Spencer rifle! With all the helling around he had been to, not one good blow had he struck for the ranch — not one!

Might be a good thing all around if he took out his six shooter and —

That was when Tune saw the light.

It was away off there to the left someplace — the faint shine of a lamp. But the glory of it, the hope it offered, bolstered him up like a shot of red-eye. He scrubbed battered knuckles against bleared eyes and found the shine still there. It was lamplight, all right.

He stumbled toward it, muttering.

He knew very well he could have reached it easily if the confounded thing would have only stayed still, but it wouldn't. It kept dancing away just beyond his reach, first on the right of him, now on the left. Bitterly he cursed its rambling propensities. But he kept stumbling after it, lurching and staggering like a barroom drunk — even sometimes crawling. He would catch that damned light if it took all summer!

And then, finally, long ages later, he *did* come up with it. And it *was* a light — real lamplight. And it was coming from a window. A window in a building that seemed to be a ranch house.

But it wasn't Clover Cross.

It took him quite a while to realize that.

It was so damned confusing because Ives Tampa, the Clover Cross range boss, was there. Tune could see him plainly. He was sitting down in a wooden-backed chair listening to a couple fellows who seemed to be doing quite a pile of talking — real earnest turkey talking. And Tampa's face didn't seem very cheerful. And those other guys didn't look pleasant, either. Tune could not hear what they were saying, but they sure were slinging their jaws around. And it kind of seemed like he had seen those fellows before — ought to know them. Especially that short and broad one. That gent with the dark-burnt face.

Tune stood outside the lighted window and stared.

Something uncommon odd with that picture.

What was Tampa looking so dried-up about? What was he doing here if this wasn't Clover Cross? What the hell was he doing with his arms tied back of him? And if he didn't like what those gentlemen were saying — Tune sighed like a weight was pressing on him. He wished the damned building wouldn't rock so. He put an arm to the wall to steady it. To kind of hold it in place and make sure that light didn't go sneaking off again in case he closed his eyes to kind of clear them sort of.

It sure was downright odd about Ives.

Might be he had ought to go in and find out about it. Ives was his boss — remember? Ives hadn't seemed to care too much for him, but Ives was the Clover Cross boss all right — no getting around that. And *he* was the Clover Cross strayman. So if Ives was in any kind of trouble . . .

Yes, he guessed he had better go in.

He pulled his arm away from the wall. Easiest way to go in was the window. Wouldn't be much trouble to bust out a window.

He dragged out his sixgun and staggered toward it.

He had no remembrance of striking the window. He did not hear the crash of breaking glass. He *thought* he heard a sound like hoofbeats, and the figures in the room seemed oddly still and unnatural, like that windowful of dummies he had seen at Albuquerque. The dummy faces had looked a heap more real.

Funny thing about faces — take that dark fellow's mug, now. The way it was —

"Hell! That's Crowly," Tune thought. "Jess Crowly!"

Sure! And that other guy, that long lean jigger with the mismatched eyes — that was Cibecue, Crowly's ace gun slinger.

Then somebody said, "Well, damn my eyes! If it ain't the bad penny turned up again!"

That was the last thing Dakota Tune heard.

Something hard and hot clipped him side of the head and he saw yellow flame gushing out of Jess' pistol. Then the floor kind of swayed and rose up and came at him, and the window frame slapped him round the middle; and a chair came skittering across the floor and the floor caught hold of it and jabbed at him.

The lights blanked out in a burst of stars.

Chapter 22

Tune guessed rather likely he was running a fever so he wasn't much surprised that his next recollection was of a dark-haired angel with smooth cool hands who had his head in her lap and was sort of patting him or something while her salt, salt tears dropped onto his cheeks. He couldn't think what she was crying about; it made him downright uneasy. He wanted to do something about it but, about that time, she kind of drifted off from him. There came a time, however, when, opening his eyes, he saw things in their proper semblance. At least he guessed he did. He seemed to be lying in a bunk, lying flat on his back. That, anyway, was the impression he got, though he was not at all sure because all he could see was a complete vast whiteness. A heap too white for an Arizona sky. So what the hell was it? Kind of seemed like fabric and it smelled like sweat, and

It was! That's exactly what it was! It was a sheet draped over him; and his hands, kind of odd like, were folded on his chest just like he had seen them fold up a dead man's. In fact, if he'd been grabbing hold of a lily he'd have figured he *was* dead!

And then he got it. *He was supposed to be dead!*

They had got him laid out like he was in a coffin!

Cold sweat broke out of him clammily and he was about to spring up, about to dash that sheet aside in protest, when the sound of approaching voices stopped him. There were two voices, arguing. One was protesting, short and indignant; the other was a fullthroated growl. Jess Crowly's!

Booted feet clumped into the room. Spur rowels rasped the floor and stopped. There was a moment of absolute silence. Tune scarcely dared breathe. Then the resumed and nearing spur clank warned him and he let his mouth fall slackly open and prayed he would not be looked at too closely.

A hand grasped the sheet, a hand impatiently savage. The sheet was whipped away from his face and he could feel hot eyes staring skeptically down at him.

"He don't look dead to me," Crowly said, and fetched Tune a cuff with his open palm. Twice more that rough hand cuffed Tune's face, and it took all his will to keep playing dead.

Crowly let go the sheet with a grunt and turned. "He don't look dead to me," he repeated. "But we'll soon see — an' if he ain't he will be! Now then! What did you throw them shots at me fo'?"

"I have told you," Tio Felix's voice said, "we were firing at this bandido loco —"

"Never mind the lies! I reckon I know when I'm shot at! Where's the girl?"

Tune could almost feel Tio Felix cringe. But the man's voice was smooth — too smooth, Tune thought. "Quien sabe, señor — I do not know."

"By God, I've had enough of yo' lies!" Crowly rasped. Tune could hear him crossing the floor toward old Felix; and only the remembrance of the gangling Cibecue prevented him from going at once to the old man's assistance. It was hard, bitter hard, to lay in that bunk and know that Jess Crowly's back was turned and still do nothing about it.

But he stayed where he was, luckily.

And a moment later he was glad he had, for the man came stamping in. He said, "I've looked all over this goddam place and I can't find a sign of her. She's got away, right enough!"

"How *could* she git away?" Crowly snapped. "How *could* she git away? Her hawss is still out theah. The only two people she's interested in — Did you look in the feed bins? Git back then an' look in 'em! And *look* this time! Don't come back heah without her! If you haven't the wit t' do any betteh, git a lantern an' track her down — git the dawgs!"

Tune heard the gun fighter go clanking off; then the sound of a blow — Tio Felix's protest. Crowly snarled, "You talk an' talk quick or I'll break ev'y bone you got in you!"

There was that in Crowly's voice that warned Tune. The man was in a fit mood for murder. Events that for awhile had marched according to Crowly's slightest whim were threatening now to get out of hand and the man was reverting to natural instincts. This war was not going just the way he had planned it, and the two-bit outfits clinging by their teeth to the skirts of this thing were showing an unexpected stubbornness in their rabbity refusal to do the expected. They were not ganging up on Jess. They were taking their beatings like yellow curs, and Jess wanted action. Action to make it look like the Seven Keys outfit was being forced to take things into their own hands to save themselves. Even Tune had not acted as Jess had thought he would. He had not run Felix's sheep off or slaughtered them; he had not made one overt move that Jess could exploit to his own advantage. Only the girl had played into Jess' hands; and Tune didn't know this. But he saw that the veneer of easy tolerance was gone from Jess. Time could defeat him. Crowly must force the issue or admit himself licked. An empire lay within his grasp and he was not the man to lose it calmly.

Tune sensed something of this in the mood of the man; it was in the timbre of Crowly's voice. Unless Felix talked Jess Crowly would kill him. Crowly was done with fooling, and with bluffing. He was going to batter the old man senseless; from Jess' point of view Felix's use was ended. So far as Jess was concerned he had not *been* any use!

Felix said, as though recognizing this, as though only now he were realizing his peril, "What would you have me tell you, señor? What —"

"You can tell me wheah that damn' gel's got to!"

Crowly's talk wasn't nearly so careful now. With the baring of his baser self Crowly wasn't keeping up his Southern drawl; even his accent was frequently missing. His words were clipped, his tone grown ugly. There was no sign now of the cool crafty schemer who had hoodwinked Stokes and Stacey Wilkes. This was the real Crowly talking — the man Jess had striven so long to hide.

Without guessing Crowly's past Tune sensed these things; they were there in the man's tone of voice and look.

Tune carefully lifted the sheet back off him but Felix's scared eyes gave the move away and a pistol, placed beneath the sheet, fell noisily off the bunk to the floor.

Jess Crowly slewed his dark face around and his cold jawed mouth twitched downward wickedly as his brown right fist blurred up with a gun. Tune could see the hammer go whacking back and the lurid flame that burst from its muzzle. But the flame went up and into the rafters and its lead went harmlessly through the roof as Tio Felix, springing, got his arms like a vise around Jess Crowly and bore him backward in a cursing fall.

Some remote recess of Tune's spinning mind knew an instant of wonder for the man's brash courage; but he had no time to think of it then. He must find the gun he had knocked from the bunk. He must get his hands on it quickly; for even now he could hear the pounding boots of the hurrying Cibecue.

He saw the gun's shine in the light of the lamp. It lay just under the edge of the bunk, and Tune dropped down and bent to get it. Yet, even as he grasped its worn-smooth butt, the lamp wildly flared to a sixgun's explosion, and his backward thrown look saw Felix teetering on buckling knees. The sound of the old man's fall was lost in the trip-hammer blasts of Crowly's gun. Tune could hear the thwack of Jess' bullets round him, but the man's ragged nerves wouldn't waste time for aiming. He was firing blindly, in the grip of fury, firing as fast as he could fan the hammer.

Tune threw one shot and saw dust jump from Crowly's vest; but Jess wasn't much hurt, he was gone on the instant, whirled away through the doorway in tumultuous flight. A hall hurled back the sound of his leaving — a sound suddenly lost in the crash of impact. A gun went off in that outside dark and Cibecue's voice cried, "Gawd A'mighty!" Then Tune was at the door, pistol lifted; but they both were gone. There was nothing to shoot at.

Feverishly Tune plucked shells from his belt. He was fumbling them into the pistol when presentiment gripped him, a premonition of danger so acute and strong it was almost as though he heard Larinda's voice calling over the empty miles to him. It froze him there in his tracks, tense and staring.

Every urge of his blood bade him fly to her side — bade him larrup across the hills to find her; but he stood where he was and finished loading the pistol. There were things here he must see to first if he would truly aid her. He must find Ives Tampa and if he was ever to make any security for her he must seek out and kill Jess Crowly — he *must!* It was all very suddenly very beautifully clear; it was as simple as that, *he must kill Jess Crowly!*

As the lightning sweeps the dark aside, so the webs of doubt were swept out of Tune's mind and he saw the issue as it really was. He must kill Jess Crowly.

The Clover Cross fight was one for survival, the last desperate stand of a grand old ranch struggling for life, for continuance, battling the powers of greed that would seize and destroy it. It was, in Tune's eyes, the magnificent courage and pluck of one girl pitted against an unscrupulous wolfpack. There was no choice for Tune if he would help Larinda. He must locate Jess Crowly and kill him, for naught but Jess' death could stop this.

Gun loaded and ready he was about to go catfooting down the dim hall when a voice, softly coming from the room he had left, wheeled him round in his tracks with widesprung eyes.

It was the blue eyed girl, the gitana, Panchita.

Chapter 23

Straight and slim she stood with the lamp-glow back of her, with its yellow shine streaming through her hair, with her frail arms braced against the sides of the door.

Always, he thought, she had come like this, unexpected and sudden as a face from the fog. It occurred to him, ironically, that all their contacts had begun this way, with the two of them, motionless, staring back at each other. He tried to make out her face and catch what emotion was enlivening her features, but could not. The light was against him, shining full upon him; and he wondered what she saw, if her child's eyes could see through the fight scars and grime to the man he had been, to the deep solid core of him. And if they could, what they found there — if what they found seemed worth having.

It was a curious thought in that time and place. Yet it seemed to him to be of great import, a thing he needed to know; and still it did not occur to him to wonder why or how her opinion could matter.

She said: "Please — will you come now and look at him? I think — I'm afraid —"

Tune pulled himself out of his thinking and followed her into the lamplit room. Felix lay where he had fallen, grotesquely sprawled, unmoving, a dark stain clotting the goods of his shirtfront.

Tune dropped onto his knees, but the man was dead.

Tune considered this thing with his upsweep glance taking in the drawn shades at the windows.

He met the girl's eyes and shrugged wearily. Hunger gnawed at his bones and he could not think when he last had eaten. He took a deep breath and got onto his feet. "We'd better get out of here."

She stood with her round eyes watching Felix. "He was a good man." She said it simply, like a benediction, and tears made a shine at the edge of her lashes. "A good man . . . but wrong. He tried to take God's judgment into his own hands. He did not understand God's ways."

She crossed herself, murmuring some phrase in Latin, and grew still with downcast eyes, silently crying.

Tune put a hand to her shoulder. She was so like a child, he thought. In her distress she was so alone. "Come, little sister

—" He spoke in Spanish, and abruptly stopped, aware that inside him something did not care to think of her that way. The words were distasteful to this inner self, and he changed them. He said, "Come — I must fetch you out of this."

But these words did not please him either. They implied an importance he did not feel. He felt humble when he thought of this girl. It was odd . . . And he felt inadequate to console her. Words were but sounds, and one suffering such loss did not want sounds. Words were pads strung together to cushion life's ways for the timid. This gitana was not timid; she had strength and character. He hadn't thought of that before; but she had these and she cried, not out of weakness, but for love.

And he wondered, strangely, if she would cry for him.

When he spoke his tongue felt thick and unwieldy. "What will you do now without your uncle? Who will you go to? Have you someone . . ."

She came to him. She clung to him, wetting his shirt with her tears.

He patted her clumsily, acutely conscious of his extreme inadequacy. Strange thoughts and stranger feelings touched him; and he winced when he thought of

Tune, that border renegade, that plaything of destiny, trying to comfort this stricken child. Tune, the leather slapper — that gunsmoke king of corpse-makers! It was almost blasphemy!

But Panchita clung to him, and he did not put her away from him though time was a-wing and time was precious. She clung to him fiercely and a kind of comfort came of this union, and then she pounded his chest with her fist. "Oh, Mother! Mother Mary!" she cried through her sobs, "— Guide me! Guide me!" And she clung to Dakota more tightly, tight as death, with her tear-wet face squeezed against his shoulder.

Then, abruptly, she was staring up at him — was pulling his head down, hesitantly. In the manner of a child she touched her lips to his face. And, more suddenly still, she caught his rough face in both her hands and, fiercely, almost defiantly, she kissed him hard on the mouth; and stood back.

"I will go with *you*," she said breathlessly.

Chapter 24

There were many things Tune needed to know, but the answer to that was not one of them. He looked at her, and the eyes he suddenly snatched away were haunted eyes and hunted. A sound broke groaningly out of him and he wheeled away lest she sense the cause and divine the depth of his misery. Better by far had he never seen . . . He *could* not take her — he *dared* not. Ives Tampa had put the name to him. "Gun handy," Tampa had called him; and that was the way all the world must see him — a hardcase gunman without compunction.

"You can't!" he said, keeping his eyes away from her. He spoke through clenched teeth and the words came out harshly.

She looked at the back of his head. Her lips trembled.

"I would be very quiet — I could keep out of sight."

"It ain't that, Panchita — You don't understand. You — I'm a chaparral rat — a man wanted for murder — an outlaw with a price on his head!"

"Oh, but that —" she said; then she looked at him oddly and stopped. "Don't you think I could be a chaparral rat, too? I've lived in the brush with Tio Felix —"

"Living with your uncle —"

"Oh, but he wasn't — I mean, not really. Only by courtesy —"

"I couldn't even be a fake uncle to you!"

She looked at him quickly and, tremulously, smiled. "Don't leave me, Dakota. Don't *ever* leave me —"

"You're a child. You don't unders—"

"I am not a child! I'm eighteen!" She said indignantly: "Of course I understand. Your'e trying to protect me from stuffy conventions — from what people might say — from what they would think. What do you suppose they are thinking now? Convent bred and in the brush with old Felix!"

She came nearer, laid her hand on his arm. "Dakota, life can be good or it can be very bad — life is what any one of us makes it. Life is a *personal* responsibility; it usually becomes whatever you think it is. For two years I thought it was terrible — looking back on it now I am not so sure. God works His will in strange guises, but belief will help. If you *believe* you are right — I mean *honestly* believe it — what matters it what the world may think? What is the world but a lot of foolish rumors? — a lot of bewildered people very strangely like ourselves, Dakota."

Tune stared, baffled.

As though she would clinch the matter she said, and quite seriously, "I am old enough to know my own mind —"

"Then you're old enough to know better!"

"Lots of girls are wedded and bedded —"

"Good God!" Tune cried. "*I* can't marry you!" Then his cheeks got red and he scowled and fell silent. "Would you want to live with an *outlaw?* — with a fellow who's killed an' will probably kill more?"

"What has that got to do with it? Where there is love —"

"Love! What kind of love do you think *I* could give you?"

She was silent a moment, looking down at her feet. "I suppose it's the waiting that's always the hardest —on the woman, I mean. But I've lived two years with that kind of waiting —"

Tune said midway between a groan and a snort, "Come on! We've got to find Tampa — we've got to get out of here!"

But she stood there, unmoving. Color got into her cheeks. "I didn't ask you to *marry* me — only to let me go with you. I could make myself useful. There would be clothes to mend and meals to be cooked —"

"More than half the time there wouldn't *be* any meals. Come! We've argued enough —"

"Am I so ugly, then? Do you find me so hard to look at?"

Tune groaned, and his clenched fists tightened till the bones shone white through his skin. A pressure of months was bursting in him, all the hard ways of his life cried out and he knew he dared stand there and talk no longer.

He said harshly, "We'll argue this later. Ives Tampa —"

"He's gone — if you mean that man who was tied in the chair. We looked. The ropes had been cut; the man was gone. There was blood on the chair . . ."

Tune thought: *They've killed him. They've killed him and hidden his body to make it look like he's quit the country.*

"Then we'd better get out of here."

But it was the girl that made their leaving imperative. He would rather have stayed to hunt for Jess Crowly — to hunt for Jess Crowly and kill him. It was a bitter thought, but Jess' death was all that could now save Clover Cross; and Larinda

McClain was depending on him. And she had that right, for he'd passed his word. But he had to get Panchita out of here.

It was all kind of mixed up and complicated. Even in his mind it was complicated — especially in his mind. There was that knife-handy killer to be reckoned with, the man who had killed Stacey Wilkes and Teal and now was trying his damndest to get this girl. If you could just take the job one thing at a time; but a man never could. Life didn't run that way in this world. Like goodness and badness it was all mixed up till no one but God knew the straight of it.

He said, "Where are the horses?"

She gave him a small little smile like a child might have offered a bit of striped candy and turned through the door and led off down the hall that was like a black tunnel dug straight to the pit.

Tune followed, recalling again that unexplained shot he had heard in the town just before Stacey Wilkes had killed young McClain. That shot, he guessed now, had been fired at Panchita. By that same man he'd fought with, probably. That fellow was sure out to get her all right — but *why?* What did she know that they didn't want told? What had she seen with her so-blue eyes? Who was she? No common gypsy, certainly — they didn't raise gypsies in the quiet of a convent!

Tune closed the kitchen door screen softly.

It would soon be light. The night was fled and, already, dawn's crimson banners were burning up into the eastern sky. Sunrise would soon be upon them. It was time to be gone — it was past time.

Tune's glance raked the roundabout buildings. There was too much quiet in this yard; it rasped across Tune's nerves like a file.

He moved after the girl toward a thicket of squatting cedar. Jess Crowly and Cibecue would be somewhere close . . . somewhere close, sharply watching with rifles. He could tell by the feel of his cringing muscles. Crowly wasn't the kind to pass up any bets.

Of a sudden Panchita stopped and whirled toward him.

"Look!" she cried, catching hold of his arm — his good arm. And Tune, swinging his head, discovered that Crowly had not been idle. They had talked too long. The whole back wall of the house was aflame! Dried by the years it burned like tinder. Already the flames were spreading and twisting; glass was falling from the windows in sheets; and Tune cursed. He saw in this Jess Crowly's answer to the small ranchers' lack of aggressiveness. They had failed to strike back as Crowly had wanted, so now he was striking back for them. He was burning his place and he would raise hell about it; he would use this fire to fine advantage. And if Ives Tampa's body were found in the ruins . . .

Something, whacking the ground, flung sand on Tune's boots; and he caught the girl's arm, started running. He knew what had thrown that sand without guessing and, as though in confirmation, a rifle slammed sound from a bunkhouse window.

"Quick!" he cried, pushing the girl toward the cedars. "Get under cover!" He thumbed a wild shot at the bunkhouse, well knowing the range was too great for a pistol.

Panchita let out a stifled cry and Tune, pounding into the thicket, found her crouched on the far side peering through the dark mass of the branches, staring wide eyed at a pair of tied horses.

There was dismay in her glance. "They've moved them — the horses, prala! We tied them in here —"

Tune nodded. His eyes were sharply probing the shadows, the flame-harried shadows of a low line of timber some dozen or so feet beyond the tied horses. They were buckskins and good ones. They were hitched to a stump and the stump was a long forty feet from Tune's station. A smart man would have hidden those broncs, but what Jess Crowly had done was more smart. He had left them in sight, knowing Tune would try for them. And while Tune tried Jess would not be idle.

"I'll have to get them," Tune grunted.

"But you *can't*. They'll kill you — that's what they *want!*"

"Sure. But we can't get away from here without horses."

And that was the plain hard truth of it. And to remain much longer in this thicket would be suicide. Time was with Jess Crowly. Time was what Jess wanted right now; time for his men to see that fire and come running. It was possible Tune couldn't reach those tied horses, but —

"You can't!" wailed Panchita. "They'll kill you!"

"They'll try," Tune said. He grinned toughly. "They'll try whether I go for them horses or not. Mebbe I'll be lucky —"

"No!" There was a very real fright, a very real concern, in the dark haunted eyes that looked back at him. "I will not *let* you go!"

Tune smiled at her then, smiled compassionately. "Don't you see? Don't you get it, Panchita? This is what it is like to be tied to an outlaw. This is the kind of life you would share with me. Buck up now — stick your chin out, pardner . . . That's more like it. Stay here now and help me. I've got to have a free mind to get those horses. You stay put where I'll know where to find you."

He patted her shoulder; shoved fresh loads in his pistol. Six chances to live if he could dodge their lead. Six chances to go out with company.

One of those two, Jess Crowly or Cibecue, would be watching for him now, watching for him to make this break, wickedly watching across the sights of that rifle. The other would be up ahead there someplace, probably in that timber just beyond the tied horses.

But there wasn't any way he could do this differently.

He had to get those horses.

It was neck meat or nothing.

Chapter 25

The flames roared with the sound of a high wind. Sparks and bits of exploding planking fell through the resinous branches and set up little spirals of smoke; and one piece, about the size of a quarter, flaked down on Tune's hat and ate through its brim with a smell of scorched hair.

Tune raked the timber with his hard gray eyes. He saw no sign of movement, no glint of weapons. No scolding bird gave the man's place away, and yet Tune's judgment told him there would be a man someplace in that stilldark undergrowth, and the man would fire soon as Tune left cover.

Bitterly Tune's glance went back to the horses.

A blue whistler jerked the crown of his hat and left a new part in the hair at his temple and the sound of the rifle slammed out of the harness shed.

So the man in the bunkhouse had quit his post. Either that or this had been the second man firing, and Tune didn't quite believe that. It would not be like so good a general as Jess to pass up the timber, to have no man there to stop Tune.

It was anyone's guess but the truth was needed.

Heat from the house was like a breath from Hell's furnace.

Tune changed position and another slug screamed, dropping twigs from near branches. Rifle sound lashed from a rain barrel midway between the harness shed and this thicket.

The man was closing in. Or maybe — but Tune hoped not — some of the Seven Keys crew had arrived.

Tune parted the branches, flung a look at the girl. "Take care of yourself," he said, and was gone.

Two forty-fives drummed lead from a treetop, hammering the ground with its thuds all around him. One shot withered past his cheek; then another. He glimpsed the wild roll of the tied horses' eyes. One of the pair suddenly reared up, snorting; and Tune groaned, certain the reins wouldn't ever hold it. He drove his legs madly but was still out of reach when the strained leather parted.

The horse went into the air like a rocket.

Tune, keening the trees with bitter eyes, saw muzzle light break through a dense clump of foliage, briefly disclosing the sniper's dark shape; and Tune fired on the instant and a man came crashing down through the branches. The loose horse lunged toward Tune and he hurled himself at its neck in swift tackle, and one hand caught in the cheekstrap and held, and he threw all his weight into dragging that head down.

The frightened horse stopped, blowing hard through its nostrils. It flung its hind legs up, pitching. Tune caught the horn and let go of the cheekstrap. Around and around they went, the horse squealing and kicking, before Tune got a leg finally over the saddle. The rain-barrel rifle was bang-banging frantically when the girl, all wild-flying hair and bare legs, swept past Tune on the other buckskin.

How long they rode, or how far, did not matter. All that mattered was the gaining of distance, the putting of miles between them and the roaring inferno of Wilkes' Seven Keys Ranch. The sun was well up when they finally stopped on a low rise of ground and quested the long roll of prairie before them. A huddle of buildings ten miles due west showed a spatter of white against the dun hills.

"Clover Cross," Panchita said, pointing.

Tune thought a moment, debating the wisdom of taking her there. There was no real reason why he should not, of course. Larinda could put the girl up; would probably be glad to. And right now, he thought, while they breathed their horses, would be a good time to get a few of those answers which had so long been eluding him.

He said, "How'd you happen to show up when you did? — I mean, back there at Seven Keys after I'd passed out."

"It was Tio Felix," she said. "When I told him how Jess Crowly was using him, he refused to believe it. I offered to bring him to you so that he could see that button you found in Grankelmeir's stable, but he would not listen. He started right out for Seven Keys to see Jess; he seemed sure Jess would admit it if it were so. So of course I came with him. We were just riding up when we saw you smash that window. I guess we flogged up our horses. Jess must have heard us — he probably thought all Clover Cross was coming. Both he and that cross-eyed fellow were gone when we came in and found you. You were lying half across the window sill, kind of folded there, stunned. There was an overturned chair with some blood on it, and another chair all broken up on the floor just under you."

"But you didn't see Tampa?"

She shook her head, pushed the black hair out of her eyes again.

"We saw him through the window just before you smashed the glass, but not afterwards. When we got inside he wasn't there, just the blood — like I've told you. We came in through the kitchen. They could have left some other way."

"I reckon they've done for old Ives," Tune muttered.

He cleared his throat, looked at her. His face was thoughtful, embarrassed also. "Where did you come into this mess? There's a powerful lot of things I'd like to know about you — you're no common gypsy —"

"Why not? What's the matter with me?"

He ignored the so-innocent look of her eyes. "Your language, for one thing. You don't talk like a gypsy — you've been educated. Didn't you tell me you were raised in a convent? I'll admit you had me fooled for awhile, but you're not gitana — gypsies aren't brought up in convents. You're a Texan, aren't you?"

"Are there no gitanas in Texas, Dakota?"

Tune gave her a scowling look and grunted. "How did you come to fall in with Tio Felix? Who's trying so damned hard to kill you? — and why? Who was that fellow I saw you fighting with in front of Riske Quentin's? Was he the man that was after you last night?"

Her eyes laughed back at him. "So many questions!"

"Yeah. And I've got a lot more that I'd like to get answered." He looked at her blackly, scowled and grunted. "You got me fightin' my hat for sure. First time I see you is outside a Tucson sportin' house, tryin' to fight off a man with a knife. Then I see you in Oro Blanco, fightin' another guy. Then you're following me up on a store porch and high-and-mightily telling me to fork over a button I found in a stable. You don't get the button, but a couple hours later you go out of your way to fetch me a horse I'm needin' so bad I could taste it. And that ain't all! I give Lou the slip and get out of there. Then I find you guarding a sheep camp that's got no sheep and nobody in it but old Tio Felix. Then I come back to Blanco and you're there, too, hollerin' for help again, like usual. But first, you let out a shout that saves my bacon; then you're off, dashing into the desert, with half the scum of the town foggin' after you. Then I find you with a guy trying to break your neck. What

244

is it you've got?" He gave her a baffled scowl. "I don't get it!"

She laughed at the comical look of him. Then the gayness faded. Her eyes grew sober and searched his face. "Perhaps it is those buttons, prala."

"Buttons!" He looked at her. "You're pretty sharp, ain't you. How'd you know I'd got hold of another one?"

"But you told me — just a moment ago you said *'those buttons.'* Anyway, I saw you jerk it off of his chaps. He was wearing those same moleskin chaps when he killed Teal and Wilkes — at least, I *think* he was. I saw them plainly after Teal was killed."

"Then you know who he is!" Tune exclaimed excitedly. "You know — Hell! — beggin' your pardon, ma'am; I mean, that's why he's been tryin' to kill you, of course!"

"I'm not sure. It *might* be."

"Huh!" Tune gave her a slanchways look and grunted. "I suppose I'll know all about it some day — if I live long enough. Don't hurry it none on *my* account, but when you get round to it give me the nod. It's Crowly, ain't it?"

"I *think* it's Crowly."

"What's that? Didn't you just get through saying you saw him wearin' those moleskin chaps?"

"I didn't say that, exactly. I didn't see him when Wilkes was killed — I wasn't near Wilkes when he died. But I *did* see Jess coming out of the stable that day, and he was wearing them then. I mean the day Teal was knifed. I *think* it was Jess — anyway, it was somebody wearing those moleskin chaps, and I saw Jess once with them on."

Tune sighed. "Look — do it over. Start with Teal. What were you doing in the stable that time?"

"I wanted to talk with you, privately — I mean, I didn't want to be seen with you, because that would have meant putting you under the same threat . . . Anyway, I hurried to the stable, figuring you would go there — I mean, after I left you outside of Riske Quentin's. I meant to wait in the stable till you showed up. I slipped in through the back; but just as I did a man brushed past me, leaving. Going out the back way. He was walking fast, not making any sound. I saw the chaps but not the man's face. It was later I saw those chaps on Jess Crowly. He was wearing them when he shot Wink Parr —"

"My God!" Tune said. "Who's Wink Parr?"

"He was the man I was struggling with at Riske Quentin's. He was trying to persuade me to go back home. You remember when Wilkes shot that boy at the hotel? There was a shot just before that —"

"I remember," Tune said. "I figured it was fired at you —"

"But it wasn't! Crowly fired that shot. It killed Wink Parr —"

"But who is this Parr?"

"He's a halfbreed Mexican who used to work for my father — he was janitor at my father's bank."

"So you *have* got a father!"

"Why, of course! I ran away from him. I ran away from home. I think my father hired Parr to find me —"

"What did you run away for?"

"At the convent one of the Sisters said my father had made plans for my future. She told me the plans; they were distasteful to me. I was to be married to a man I could not love. I didn't think my father realized my feelings. I ran away from the convent and hurried home, intending to explain my feelings and plead — Anyway, he did not know I was coming. He didn't expect me. He had company that night, a visitor — Jess Crowly. They were talking about a man, a rancher, who was going to be forced to borrow some money —"

"Does Jess Crowly know you saw him kill Parr?"

"I think so. I ran — I managed to get away. But I think he saw me; I think he tried to catch me. He chased me that night in San Saba after I heard them planning to ruin you —"

"Ruin *me!*" Tune stared, startled, unable almost to credit his ears. "To ruin *me?*"

The look of her eyes was so young and so earnest. "They called the man 'Tune' — Didn't you tell me you were wanted for a killing in Texas? Was the name of that man Sheriff Curry? — Tom Curry?"

Tune's look was incredulous. The bones of his cheeks stood out white as ivory.

Panchita looked frightened. She backed away from him.

"What — What have I said? What *is* it?"

Tune stood in his tracks, stiff-staring and frozen, searching her face with his blazing eyes. And, suddenly, there was a strange dismal feeling inside him, a sensation that was almost a pang of dismay.

"Good God!" he breathed hoarsely. "Who are you?"

"Mary Jaqueline Stokes."

Tune stood utterly still.

Mary Jaqueline Stokes!

A short ugly laugh broke across his lips.

He swung into the saddle and, without a backward look, rode off.

Chapter 26

Tune rode in a red fog of anger.

His mind was too filled with her revelations, too crowded with conjectures roused by them — too poisoned with hatred, to have any room left for charity. He thought of her, yes — but only in connection with that treacherous "friend" who had driven him into the chaparral to die. He knew this turmoil for the pestilence it was, for a gangrenous passion unworthy of him but that must ever dog his weary tracks till he faced Blackwell Stokes across the glint of a gunsight. It was a scourge of fire redly licking his veins, a spark that could flare into devastating fury whenever he permitted his thoughts to touch it. He had lived with the hope of revenge too long to discard it now, or to be swayed by things which might once have moved him. Let her look to herself! Let her try out the cure of her old man's medicine!

From the start Tune's problem had been to save Clover Cross, but they had kept him too much on the jump to get at it. Yet he might fool them all, for there still might be time to kill Jess Crowly.

And he would not have to seek Jess far.

Safford, for instance, was a gambling man; there was none of that bravo stuff mixed in Lou. He played to win and he kept his cards held close to his chest. When the deal wasn't right Lou could pass it up. He had passed many deals up and, for all Tune knew, he might be sloping right now, digging for the tules, getting out of the country. Not that Tune had accomplished so much, but because Tune, despite all the things they had thrown against him, had managed to keep going. That, from Lou's side of the table, would look rough. If it looked rough enough Lou would pitch in his hand.

But not Crowly. Jess Crowly, if Tune gauged him right, would head straight for the ranch, straight for Clover Cross. He was, Tune thought, the kind to bull his way through. Scornful of odds, Jess Crowly in the last analysis would hammer straight on. He would hammer straight on though he knew it might be the death of him, for Crowly could never admit defeat. He wasn't built that way; he couldn't bring himself to acknowledge a besting. When everything else failed, when stratagems and wiles went by the way, Jess would bull on until a bullet stopped him.

Tune was sure of this and, because he was, he felt sure dark Jess would come to Clover Cross. Jess would come to the ranch for the showdown, for the spoils or the bullet payoff. He would come if only to make sure of Tune's death.

So long as Jess had been able to keep Panchita away from Tune — and thus keep his part in Tune's ruin secret — he could have felt in no personal danger from Tune. And by this same token, all the girl's troubles — all that chasing, all those attempts made upon her life — had stemmed from the chance of her talking with Tune. Jess had figured to keep himself out of that, he had figured to let Stokes catch all Tune's vengeance.

But now Jess would know that the secret was out. Tune and the Stokes girl had gotten together and Jess would know what that could mean to him. He would have to kill Tune to protect himself.

But what had dark Jess got out of the deal? It didn't look like a man slick as Jess could ever be satisfied with the role of accomplice. A hired gun slammer in the employ of Stokes? Tune was damned if he could see Jess in *that* part. And there hadn't been any gun slamming in it, except for the shooting which had dropped Tom Curry.

Except for the shooting which had dropped Tom Curry!

Tune reared back in the saddle. He pulled up the buckskin with narrowed eyes. Had Crowly been that supposed drunken dimwit who had shot out the lights in the saloon that night? Had *Jess* dropped Sheriff Tom Curry? Was dark Jess the man?

Why, God *damn* Jess Crowly!

In the heat of that moment Tune was sure he had solved it; but as he rode on again he wasn't so sure. The role of boot-licking gun thrower didn't fit Jess Crowly with any degree of snugness. Jess was not the kind to fill a back seat when the time came for splitting the profits.

Jess was a schemer. The man who could vision what Crowly saw here — and have the brains and the guts to go after it, was hardly the man to sit calmly by while the profits of enterprise went to another. Yet, against this logic was the irrefutable fact that Tune, when he'd so trustingly borrowed that money from Stokes, had assigned his lease to the banker — to Stokes. Jess couldn't very well change that!

Tune shook his head, still baffled. If Crowly had killed Tom Curry that night — and the man was, anyway, mixed up in it — then Jess was at any rate equally responsible for the unpleasant things Tune had undergone since. For those years in the chaparral — for the blood-money price the law had put on Tune's scalp!

Maybe death and Jess Crowly wouldn't fetch the right answer.

A corner of Tune's twisted mouth twitched.

A vision had come to him out of this blackness, a vision of himself exonerated, a chance for complete restitution, for the return of his heritage — for the recapture of all those lost things he held dear.

A Jess Crowly facing a jury could talk. A dead Jess Crowly was no good to anyone . . .

The vision faded and the face of a yellow-haired girl took its place. "You will do what you have to do," she had said. She had put her trust in Tune to save Clover Cross and he had failed her miserably. So long as Jess Crowly remained alive the evil things Jess had started would go on propagating — would crawl on to fruition. Crowly's organization would carry them out. Only Jess Crowly's death could ever tip the scales.

With his jaws tightly clenched Tune rode into the yard.

There was a strange horse standing, head down, by the porch and Tune looked, oddly, a long while at it; and something turned over at the back of his mind.

A man, at that moment, stepped out of the house.

He saw Tune and stopped.

Across ten paces their eyes met and locked.

The girl had been right!

God's will took strange guises.

Chapter 27

God's will . . .

The man on the porch was Blackwell Stokes.

Stokes drew back, half starting a hand toward the bulge of the holster strapped under his coat. But he wasn't quite up to completing the gesture.

Tune's lips curled as Stokes' hand fell away.

Stokes' hooded eyes showed a terrible intentness. There was fear in the look of his waxen cheeks.

Tune said, "How are you, Blackwell — Still trimming the customers, are you?"

Stokes wet his lips several times before he could get any sound across them. "I — I had no idea you were out here, Nason. I — I suppose I should have guessed it though when Parr failed to —"

"I had nothing to do with Parr's death, Blackwell."

"You'll have a hard time convincing a jury of that."

Tune looked at him somberly.

"Perhaps it won't get to a jury," he

smiled; and the color crept back into Stokes' gray cheeks. He discarded the meaning of Tune's words for their tone and he mistook Tune's smile for an attempt at appeasement.

The wrinkles hardened about his mouth. "Your luck's played out, boy — you can't beat the law. I say you can't go on taking life with impunity! I wouldn't have your dreams for all the gold in the Denver Mint."

His shoulders managed an effective shudder. "My boy, I'm sorry for you. I would not have believed you could be so misguided. I have tried to think of you in a kinder light. It is a sad, sad thing to see a lad of your propensities — of your background and promise, go bronc in this fashion and turn against his kind. I've made allowances for you — for your youth, for the fact you'd been drinking; I tried to show Curry's death as an accident. But I was wrong —"

"I expect that's one of the things we can both agree on."

The Commissioner stared. His brows drew down, iron gray, without charity. "A man wastes his time trying to reform a blackguard!"

"I guess we can agree on that one, too.

Aren't you a little curious to learn what has happened to your daughter?"

"That lying hussy!" Stokes said: "I have no daughter! She relinquished all claim to my concern when she left my roof —"

"Then I expect Parr was out here on other business."

Tune looked at Stokes straightly.

The banker's glance slid away. "Parr! What's —" Stokes' glance came back, turned crafty. "As a matter of fact —"

"Don't bother lying," Tune said, and got out of the saddle. "I expect I can still make out to add two and two. You had Parr hunting Crowly."

"I beg your —"

"Crowly," Tune said. "Jess Crowly."

Stokes opened his mouth, but something he read in Tune's face must have scared him. He went a half step backward. He said in panic, "That lying scut's been trying to poison your mind against me!" He made a visible effort to pull himself together. "I'm going to tell you the truth! — I *did* send Parr here to hunt Jess Crowly. I was going to surprise you; I'd have let you know but I hated to awaken false hopes in your breast. I — I have reason to believe Crowly killed Sheriff Curry — I have had Parr trailing him for several months. I felt bound to prove your innocence —"

"Very kind of you, I'm sure. Is that why you had Crowly out to your house —"

"I can explain that!" Stokes cried hoarsely. "You must not believe Mary Jaqueline's lies. It was the night you applied for the loan — Crowly, acting for the Lone Star Land and Cattle Combine, came out to make me a proposition. I don't know what lies that ungrateful girl told you, but —"

"All right," Tune said. "Where's Miss McClain?"

"I beg your — Miss McClain? I don't know. I presume she's in the house —"

"Then I think we'd better be going in, also. I think she'd be interested in hearing this account."

It was very apparent Stokes did not relish the notion. But he had no choice. With a plain unease he put the best face he could on the matter and held open the door.

"After you," Tune smiled.

Sweat was a shine on the Commissioner's features. But he nodded and went jerkily into the house.

Tune followed.

Larinda McClain's look at Tune lacked interest.

"Is this the man you've been running away from?"

She spoke to Tune and the languid flick of her hand was toward Stokes.

Tune looked at her sharply.

She was very lovely in the bright morning light streaming in through the windows. Lovely, and cool with a kind of aloofness that made Tune uncomfortably conscious of his own draggled look. Her yellow hair was fresh combed and carefully contoured. The laundered starchiness of her gingham dress looked prim as her composed features and Tune found it hard to think of her as the girl he had carried so long in his thoughts — as the girl whose pleading eyes and whose promise had been so often before him through the smoke and bedlam of the cartridged past.

"Have the boys turned back that sheep —"

"I don't think I care to discuss sheep with you. While you've been helling around with that gypsy I have concluded other arrangements. You haven't answered my question. Is Mr. Stokes the gentleman you've been running away from?"

Stokes' cheeks had a little more color now.

Tune brought his look back. "I expect

you could put it that way," he said.

He hadn't remembered this room was so big. It was as though she stood far away from him. It was as though he were some casual acquaintance, some chance connection she was trying to bring into her memory. And all this thinking piled up in him, and he pulled his shoulders away from the wall and suddenly all the drive was out of him. Yet still he did not feel as he should. He was being heaved out like a wornout coat. He had ought to be angry. He'd ought to feel resentful. He felt relieved instead. It didn't seem to matter what she said to him.

"I'm to take it then you're through with my services?"

"Your services, indeed! When did I ever have them?" she said, and curled her red lips disdainfully. "I told you the way it was, before. I'm afraid we can't find a place for you here, Tune. This ranch can't afford to hire gun throwing outlaws —"

A door opened someplace at the back of the house and a man's heavy boots dragged spur sound toward them; and a man's voice said, "Larinda? I've decided to take —"

Jess Crowly came into the room and stopped.

Hate blazed out of Stokes' widening stare. His hand jerked out of his coatfront, glinting.

Crowly fired from the hip.

Yet even as Stokes staggered back he kept squeezing the trigger of that short-barreled pistol, kept throwing his lead into Crowly's braced shape as though he would smash the man down with sheer weight of it.

But it was Stokes who fell. His fingers let go their grip of the pistol. He sagged a little in the middle and teetered. He pitched suddenly forward on his face and lay still.

Jess Crowly sighed like all the breath was out of him.

Tune knew Jess was hit, but he knew the man's strength, too, and he looked for trouble. He looked at Jess' reddening shirtfront and left his gun where it was in his holster.

Crowly's face was ghastly. It was full of hard purpose. He put the flat of one hand to the wall and leaned there. He stared at Tune and drew a hard, ragged breath and, that way, still with that bracing hand to the wall, he started moving toward Tune.

"Jess," Tune said, "lie down and die decent."

"I'm —" Crowly let out a grunt. His shadow weaved wildly and he collapsed on the floor.

Tune was watching Larinda.

She pulled her eyes off Crowly. She let them come full around until she looked at Tune. She said: "Get me out of here."

He looked at her and found nothing to say. He picked up his hat and turned doorward.

"Tune! *Tune!*"

That cool expression was gone off her face now. She was running after him, just a badly scared woman still wanting her way.

"Tune!"

She caught at his arm. She tried to bar his way from the door.

"Tune — Wait! Please! Listen! Jess told me all about it — I can prove your innocence — *I can prove you didn't kill Sheriff Curry!* I can —"

Tune shook off her arms.

He went past her silently.

There was a girl dismounting in the yard outside. A ragged gitana, bare of foot, brown of face. A gypsy lass with eyes like a child's. *This* was the girl! It had been this girl all the time inside him. He knew that now. He understood now why Larinda's words hadn't mattered. He hadn't ever *cared* for Larinda. He had had to keep thinking of Larinda to get this other girl out of his mind.

But he was done with all that.

He wasn't fooling himself now.

He was going right out there and tell the girl so.